Praise for *The Hunt*

'An incredibly moving story
of feeling lost and finding
your way again'
Thompson, author of *The Rollercoaster Boy*

'clever, gentle adventure with a
masterful plot that deals
with the difficult subject of grief so
poignantly'
na Carroll, author of *The Tale of Truthwater Lake*

'Will break your heart and
mend it together again'
Piers Torday, author of *The Last Wild*

'Full of hope and beauty, and
ultimately a healing song to nature'
Hannah Gold, author of *The Last Bear*

'Brave, unforgettable and beautiful'
Lauren St John, author of *The White Giraffe*

Also By Sarah Ann Juckes
from Simon & Schuster

The Hunt for the Nightingale

THE
NIGHT
ANIMALS

First published in Great Britain in 2023 by Simon & Schuster UK Ltd

Text copyright © 2023 Sarah Ann Juckes
Illustrations copyright © 2023 Sharon King-Chai

3 5 7 9 10 8 6 4 2

Simon & Schuster UK Ltd
1st Floor, 222 Gray's Inn Road, London
WC1X 8HB

www.simonandschuster.co.uk
www.simonandschuster.com.au
www.simonandschuster.co.in

Simon & Schuster Australia, Sydney
Simon & Schuster India, New Delhi

A CIP catalogue record for this book is available from the British Library.

PB ISBN 978-1-3985-1092-0
eBook ISBN 978-1-3985-1094-4
eAudio ISBN 978-1-3985-1093-7

This book is a work of fiction. Names, characters, places and incidents are either
the product of the author's imagination or are used fictitiously. Any resemblance
to actual people living or dead, events or locales is entirely coincidental.

Typeset in the UK
Printed and Bound in the UK using 100% Renewable Electricity
at CPI Group (UK) Ltd

MIX
Paper | Supporting
responsible forestry
FSC
www.fsc.org   FSC® C171272

THE
NIGHT
ANIMALS

SARAH ANN JUCKES

illustrated by SHARON KING-CHAI

Simon & Schuster

Mum and Dad – this one's
for you
S.A.J.

For Adrian and Emma
S.K-C.

PART ONE

THE FOX

I

Night is at its deepest, darkest centre when she comes.

I'm dreaming about being stranded on a wild island when I slowly notice the paws on my chest like two solid nothings. They feel the way ice does when you hold it in your hand – like something so cold, it's just numb.

And then I open my eyes and I see her.

She has the same strange opal glow I remember them all having, but I can still make out the rust red of her coat and hungry yellow of her eyes. The glow from my nightlight is watery, but gleams off the claws pressed into my pyjama top and the tip of her nose as she sniffs me. Her black-tip ears are pointed back towards my bedroom door, listening.

Maybe I should be afraid, but I'm not. I've seen others like her before, although not for a while and never this close. They were sometimes just a rainbow haze in the sky when I was feeling lost, or a splash of colour under the surface of the swimming pool I was afraid to dive into.

But this one is here – sitting on my chest, in my bedroom, in my house, in the dead of night.

A fox. A *ghost* fox.

My heart flutters like a trapped bird.

The ghost fox is staring at me, hardly moving at all. And I'm frozen too, even though the empty pressure from her paws feels strange on my chest.

My whole house is silent as stone. There's no light under my bedroom door, which means Mum has turned everything off and gone to bed. My window is closed, so I can't hear the cars in the distance, or the wind sneaking into the shadows between tree branches. It feels like the whole world now belongs only to the ghost fox and me.

I've always wanted to see a ghost animal up close. The closest I ever got was when Dad left for India and the tiger stripes on his suitcase roared into a giant cat that sat with me and made me feel stronger. But Dad couldn't see when I pointed her out and Mum's never been able to catch any of the others either. It made me wonder if they were just something I made up.

This fox is definitely here though. As here as if she were alive. And if I didn't remember seeing ghosts before with this shimmering colour behind them, I'd maybe think that she was a living wild fox, come to scavenge the meat off my bones in the night.

'Did you come to eat me?' I whisper, just in case.

Her ears tilt forward towards my voice and she slides off my chest, so the pressure lifts. I sit up and put my glasses on, looking at her properly with her bushy tail tucked across her paws. She's still, but her outline sort of flickers with colours that collide and disappear so quickly, it's like I dreamed them.

'I'm Nora,' I whisper.

The fox tilts her head slightly, but she doesn't say her own name, because even though she's a ghost, she's still just a fox.

I feel like she's asking me a question anyway though. Something still and urgent and quietly loud that I can't hold on to.

'It must be lonely, being a ghost,' I say.

Suddenly, she leaps up, her cold-nothing paws landing on my chest again and making my heart squeeze. And I close my eyes and push through the feeling it gives me, because, yes – this is what it feels like to be alone. Cold and empty, and I already know it.

I clench my hands into fists. 'I'm strong, I'm strong, I'm strong,' I mutter, over and over again.

The pressure lifts and my caged-bird breath takes flight. But when I open my eyes, I'm just looking at an empty space where I think maybe a fox once sat.

2

It's a Good Morning today. I can tell, because Mum is
up before even I am, singing to herself in the kitchen.

Usually on Good Mornings, I stumble down the
stairs in my pyjamas before I've even put on my glasses.

But today I throw back my covers, hunting for traces
of the fox.

'Fox?' I whisper, looking into the corners of my
bedroom for a flash of rainbow, or the flick of a bushy
tail. There's nothing though – not even a strand of red
fur on my duvet, or a pawprint on my carpet.

I suppose that's not unusual. Ghosts are both here and not here, so you probably wouldn't expect them to leave anything behind. But the disappointment that it might have been a dream carves a hollow between my ribs.

'Nora?' Mum sings up the stairs. 'You up, sweetheart?'

'Coming,' I call.

I dress so fast, I put my grey school pinafore on backwards. I charge down the stairs, dropping my jumper on my school bag. Mum's already packed it for me today, so it really must be an extra-Good Morning. I run into the kitchen and hug her middle as she's buttering crumpets for my favourite poached-egg breakfast.

'Morning, sleepyhead,' Mum says, kissing the top of my head.

I press my face into her jumper. She smells like perfume and washing powder. I try to breathe it all in before it disappears like the ghost fox did.

'You want one egg or two?' she asks as she prises me off.

'Two, please,' I say, sitting at the table. She's laid it out this morning with plates and cutlery. There's orange juice with bits in and firework-bright flowers in a vase in the middle of the table.

It's been ages since we had a breakfast like this. The Bad Days seem to be happening more and more, meaning Mum's too tired to make breakfast, or too sad to get out of bed sometimes. And I'm *fine*, because I can look after myself, but seeing Mum happy this morning too makes my bones relax into my chair.

I'm annoyed that this morning is happening on a Friday and not a weekend when we could stretch into a trip to the park, or the zoo, or even just sit in the garden, so long as we're together.

'Can I stay home from school?' I ask as she sets my breakfast down in front of me.

She puts her hand on my forehead. 'Are you not feeling well?'

I shake my head. 'I just thought we could go to the zoo maybe.'

She sits down opposite me. She looks tired still. She used to have more freckles across her nose than there were stars in the sky, but they've got fainter as her skin has turned paler. Her eyes are puffy and her brown curly hair is more unbrushed than even mine is. But still she looks more like herself today.

'Maybe at the weekend,' she says. 'Is there a reason you don't want to go to school?'

I think about that for a moment. The main reason is that I have my old mum back today and I want to keep her for as long as I can. But there are other reasons too . . .

'A fox came into my room last night. I sort of want to see if she comes back.'

Mum drops her spoon and the sound of it hitting the glass table makes us both jump. 'A living fox?'

I shake my head quickly. 'A ghost, I think. You know, like the ones I saw when I was small.'

Mum lets out a relieved sort of laugh and prods my nose with the spoon. 'You had me thinking we'd had a real fox in the house for a moment.'

I dunk a bit of crumpet into my egg, slowly. 'You don't think she was real?'

She smiles, hugging her cup of tea. 'I think maybe you were having a dream. Ghosts aren't real, are they?'

I shrug and take a bite. 'Your ghosts are real though.'

Mum pinches her lips together and I wish I hadn't spoiled a Good Morning with a bad thought.

I quickly take her hand across the table. 'You're right – it was probably just a silly dream.'

She squeezes my hand, but I can see the worry building on her face.

Mum has something called PTSD, which stands for post-traumatic stress disorder. Before she was signed off work, she was a paramedic, driving around in an ambulance and saving people's lives. But then a few months ago, she started to get sad. It was like the ghosts of her day would stick around and haunt her, and they weren't rainbow-glimmered animals, but dark shadows that whispered angry things.

She explained it all to me. We sat down with the doctor together and they both let me ask questions like, *Was it something I did?* And, *How will it change things?* And, *What can I do to help?*

They told me it wasn't my fault at all. And it shouldn't change much and that Mum was still my mum, but that sometimes she might get angry or sad. The doctor said that the only thing I needed to do to help was to give Mum space when she needed it. But I can do more than that. I can protect Mum like she protects everyone else as a paramedic.

I can help make her better.

Mum kisses my hand. 'You're so grown up, baby.'

I can feel myself blushing, but it's also quite nice when she says things like that. 'I'm not a baby, Mum.'

She smiles, taking a bite of crumpet, which means she

has her appetite back today. 'Okay, *strong, independent woman*, then. It's you and me against the world, hey, pal?'

I nod, mopping up the last of my egg. It's always been just Mum and me, together. We don't need anyone else.

We can deal with everything just fine on our own.

3

I like Miss Omar, but she can be really slow at taking the class register sometimes.

The radiator under my desk is on and it makes me feel sleepy, even though it's only the start of the day and I don't think I was up for long last night. But I slump over my desk anyway, leaning on my fist, and stare out of the window.

Our classroom is on the hill, so I can see down to the war statue and the tadpole pond, across to the climbing frame and even over the playground to the football field, where some Year Fours are doing P.E. They're so far away they're just like little fleas jumping up and down.

I miss being in Year Four. The only thing you have to worry about when you're eight years old is whether you're going to score a goal, or whether the custard at lunch will have lumps in it again. Back then, I was friends with everyone in my class and we'd all play tag together at lunch, or go over to each other's houses after school.

But I can't have any of them over now. One of them might be too loud or say something that will make Mum's symptoms come back. But that's *fine* – it's easier spending lunchtimes alone so I can read my favourite books and not have to make up excuses about Mum, or me.

My eyelids are getting heavy and I'm feeling warm in my school sweater, so the skin on my back itches.

I blink slowly, and just before my eyes close all the way I see a rainbow-smudged tail disappearing behind the weeping cherry tree next to the pond.

I jolt upright so fast I knock my pencil case off the desk and Miss Omar stops halfway through a 'good morning'.

'Nora, can you not throw your pencils, please?'

My face is red-hot now and I know I should pick my case up from the floor, but instead I'm just searching the outside for my ghost fox.

I'm up from my chair slightly and some of the others on my table have noticed and are looking now too, even though they don't even know what they're looking for. But once they look, everyone looks, and soon all my old friends are running to the window, searching the empty outside for something I know none of them will be able to see.

'Class 5O – back to your seats!' Miss Omar shouts, clapping her hands, but also craning her own head to look too. Everyone mumbles and mutters back to their desks, some of them looking at me strangely. But I don't care and keep my eyes outside.

I'm sure I saw it. A fox's tail with the same rainbow edges I remember from last night.

I sit fidgeting in my seat for the whole lesson after that, not even putting my hand up to answer questions in science that I know the answers to, because of all the stories Mum's told me about fixing femurs and mending metacarpals.

As soon as it's break-time, I burst out of the classroom and onto the playground without even getting my coat, even though it's starting to rain. I stand there for a moment, turning round on the spot, looking for a hint of rainbow as the others in my class bustle past me.

'Nora! Nora, come play football with us,' Saffie says, tugging on my arm.

'Tag – you're it!' Rachael says, tapping me on the back.

I shrug them both off, my chest feeling cold for a moment – just like it did under the ghost paws last night. Then I see her – tearing like a comet with a rainbow trail across the playground.

I take off running, raindrops splattering dotted lines on my glasses. I squint through them, my breathing huffy, blood fizzing with excitement. My feet hit tarmac as the fox glances back towards me, panting. And my eyes are so fixed on her that I don't spot the boy in my way until I'm running right into him.

'Hey!' he shouts as my shoulder barges into his pointy one, making him drop the ball he was holding.

'Sorry, sorry,' I say, my eyes still on the fox now disappearing under the branches of the weeping cherry tree by the pond.

I pick up the ball and hold it out for him to take. But instead of taking it, the boy shoves me, so his pointy shoulder rams back into mine.

I blink, stumbling backwards.

Some of the children around us stop to watch,

whispering behind their hands. I frown at the boy who shoved me – a boy in the other class in my year called Joel, with a pinched expression and a dirty chin. His face is bright red, like he might explode.

'Why don't you watch where you're going?' he shouts, bashing the ball out of my hands so it bounces, angrily.

'Sorry—' I go to say again, but some of the others in my class start gathering round me, all shouting their own things over me.

'Leave her alone, Joel.'

'She said she was sorry already.'

My back prickles angrily. 'I don't need any help,' I mutter.

Joel clenches his fists and starts shouting again – this time at them – and soon the whole school seems to be shouting at each other and their voices make my breath catch in my throat.

It reminds me of the last time Mum and I went to the supermarket together. She picked me up after school and I held the list whilst she put things in the basket. And everything was fine, until a group of teenagers came in, shouting loudly. They weren't saying angry things, but the noise made all the colour drain from Mum's face,

as loud noises like that can make her PTSD symptoms come out in full force.

I feel like all the colour has drained from me now, too. I stumble round them, my trainers slipping and sliding over the grass towards the weeping cherry tree, looking for traces of rainbow.

'Please, Fox,' I whisper. 'Make me stronger, like the other ghost animals did before.'

There's a beat where the rain comes down heavier and

the shouting turns to the squeals of children running inside.

'Pssst! In here!' a voice says from inside the dome of branches fountaining out from the trunk in the centre.

'Fox?' I squeak, my thoughts racing. 'But you're just—'

'Quickly!' the voice says again. 'Before the teachers see.'

I peer through the branches at the shape crouching in the middle, looking for her shimmery colours. But then a hand thrusts out between the branches and drags me inside where a boy with short Afro hair and a camouflage coat is staring at me with wide eyes.

'Are you okay?' he says. 'I saw Joel barge into you – he's always doing things like that to me, too.'

'I'm *fine*.' I wriggle out of his grip, looking at the dome of branches around us. It's like a whole other world in here. The shouting in the playground has dropped away and all I can hear is my own quick breaths and the gentle patter of rain on the tree. I can see branches with small buds growing all around me, framing the twisted trunk in the centre and the boy, staring at me like there's something wrong when there isn't.

'You're Nora, aren't you? Nora Frost, from 5O?'

I ignore him, looking around the bottom of the tree

where the trunk is bursting through the paving stones and the roots have made them flip onto their sides.

The ghost fox isn't anywhere to be seen, so I push past the boy to the outside again, looking around at the blurs of other children, running with their cardigans held over their heads, back into classrooms to escape from the rain. I see grey playground and grey clouds and grey uniform – but no rainbow fox.

There's a rustle from behind me and a hand closes on my wrist again, pulling me back into the arms of the tree.

'What are you *doing*?' he says. 'It's raining. If the teachers spot us, we'll have to go inside.'

'Stop pulling me around.' I yank my wrist from his grip. The top of the tree tangles into my hair and my back prickles with heat. 'You scared her away,' I say, a bit louder than I meant to.

The boy takes a step back, looking around. 'Who?'

I huff, wrestling my hair from the tree. I want to storm back out again and keep looking, but the boy's right. The rain outside the tree is hammering into the pavement now and I can hear the far-off sound of the dinner ladies calling the stragglers inside. And even though I usually like rained-off playtimes now, because I can just sit and read and not be told off for not playing with anyone else, I don't want to go back inside. Not yet.

I squat down again, my eyes still hunting for rainbows.

The boy is staring at me. 'Were you supposed to meet a friend here or something . . . ?'

I don't look at him. I don't want to tell him about the fox. Not because I'm embarrassed, but because it's better not to tell people about these things. It's the same with Mum's diagnosis. As soon as people know about her PTSD, their faces change. They get all sympathetic and like something is really wrong, when it isn't.

I don't say anything and neither does he. He just stares at me like he's reading me, like I'm a book whose pages are open. The rain comes down harder and harder, but the silence inside the tree feels like its own curtain of noise.

'I'm Kwame James,' he says, finally. 'I'm in 5R. I think you live opposite my grandad Erwin. I'm there all the time; I see you riding your bike.'

I don't say anything, so he carries on.

'This is my secret hideout – do you like it? I come in here every break-time to escape Joel. You can stay in here too though if you want? I don't mind.'

He squints at me and I try not to look at him.

'If you're being bullied too, we can stick togeth—'

'Look,' I say, quickly. 'It's nice of you to invite me into your hideout. But I'm *fine* on my own.'

Kwame grins suddenly, huge dimples appearing in each of his cheeks like moon craters. And I notice that his eyes are the same kind of swirled-up brown as the tree trunk behind him. 'Me too! Hey – maybe we can be fine on our own together? I know some games we can play, or you can choose if you want.'

I sigh loudly, scrunching up my eyes. Outside, I hear the whistle from the dinner ladies again.

'Just – just leave me alone, please,' I say.

I pull back the curtain of branches, and I run.

4

I know as soon as I burst from the cycle path onto my road after school, that the Good Morning has turned into a Bad Afternoon.

The terraced houses on my street curve down the hill into the distance. All the front doors are brown or white or grey – except ours. Ours is bright red – the same colour as my bike. Mum and I painted it last year and it's wonderful, but it also makes it clear all the way from the corner when there's a white note pinned to the front of it waiting for me to get back from school.

I squeeze my brakes and take as long as possible to ride the last bit to the front door, and even longer to put my bike away in the shed we built in the front garden, next to the wheelie bins. In no time at all though, there's only the note left to read, with my name in Mum's shaky handwriting.

Nora,

I'm sorry, pal, I'm not feeling well again. Perhaps you can go round Saffie's for dinner?

I love you.

Mum x

I stare at the kiss next to her name and wish I could feel it on me in real life.

Saffie is one of the girls in my class that I used to play with. At the beginning, I would go to her house to give Mum space when the symptoms were bad. Saffie lives with her mum and dad in a big house and they all eat pierogi dumplings and Polskie naleśniki, which are what they call pancakes in Poland. And afterwards we'd ride our bikes up and down her road until there was no light left and it was time to go home.

I don't really talk to Saffie any more, just like I don't talk to anyone else in my class either. When I was at her house, I heard her whispering with her parents about my mum and asking whether she's okay. And I started to notice that she would always let me win in races and would speak to me really quietly, like I might get a fright otherwise. And I know she was being kind, but I didn't like it. I'm *fine* and Mum is *fine* and everything is *fine*. I don't need to go to their house any more, even if Mum still thinks I do.

I open the door quietly and tiptoe into the living room. Mum has left the TV on and I wonder if maybe that was what brought on the Bad Afternoon. Sometimes it can be something someone says, or a loud noise like in the supermarket that time, or sometimes it will happen all on its own.

I turn the TV off and stand at the bottom of the stairs, listening.

Mum's bedroom door is closed and the whole house is quiet. Once upon a time, her door was always open. She'd leave it ajar for me, so I could come in if I had a nightmare, pulling me into her bed and hugging me tight. She'd let me warm my cold feet on her hot ones and whisper in my ear.

'You are brave, Nora. You are the strongest person I know.'

I grip the note she left for me tight and close my eyes.

I feel the cold nose sniffing at my tiger-striped socks before I see her. My ghost fox.

My stomach flips. Tiptoeing into the living room, I close the door behind her as she slips in after me and does a running jump onto the sofa.

'You're here,' I whisper.

The ghost fox tucks her tail across her paws, her rainbow edges racing purple and green and red. My heartbeat sounds too loud for the quiet house, so I sit down on the other side of the cushions, staring at the light fur on her chest, the squint of her eyes and the scar stretching across her muzzle.

I put my hand out to stroke her and her ears flick back, looking for a moment like she might jump off the sofa and run away.

'No!' I say, louder than I should with Mum asleep upstairs. I wince, lowering my voice to a whisper. 'Don't leave. Can you stay with me? Please?'

The ghost fox doesn't answer; she just stares at me and the note in my hand telling me to go to Saffie's house.

I shake my head. 'I'm *fine* here, promise. But . . . if you can sit with me, maybe that might be nice.'

The ghost fox tilts her head to the side and my insides feel cold and empty again, like her paws are back on my chest. She doesn't leave though. I put on some cartoons with the subtitles on and the sound off and she watches them with me. I do my homework at the table, and she curls up at my feet. And when my stomach rumbles, she follows me into the kitchen as I follow the instructions to heat up a microwave lasagne, even though Mum doesn't really like me cooking dinner on my own. I'm getting good at it now though.

I stop the microwave before it pings and put the lasagne onto three plates – one for me, one for Mum, and one for the ghost fox, who sneezes when she sniffs it. And then I write Mum a note, tucking it carefully under the plate and leaving it outside her bedroom door, for when her sadness lets her go for long enough to remember that she's hungry.

Mum,

I love you, too.

Nora x

I keep expecting the ghost fox to disappear on me again, but she doesn't. She stays all through my dinner, even though she doesn't eat any of her own – maybe because ghost foxes don't need to eat. And when I go to bed, she curls up on the carpet of my room.

'Thank you for staying with me,' I whisper.

Her yellow eyes stare at me like she sees into that cold place in my chest where I feel alone, even though I'm *fine*. I chose it to be this way, after all. I reach my hand out again from my bed towards her and, this time, she leans forward very slightly to push her cold-nothing forehead once into my palm.

5

Dawn is sneaking in behind my curtains when I wake up from a dream about a sea with huge waves, trying to turn me over. My heart is already beating so fast it feels like it might burst from my chest, when I roll over and come face to face with the ghost fox – up on my bed and panting, so her sharp teeth gleam in the new-morning light.

I yell out and then quickly slap my hand over my mouth to stop the sound waking Mum. The ghost fox dances around in a circle on the bed, so her empty-heavy paws make me feel empty-heavy inside. I fumble for my glasses and sit up as she jumps back off the bed.

She's still here – even though I'm definitely not dreaming any more. Her colours seem to be racing today too, flicking green, or maybe blue, or maybe purple and red. She's not just staring still at me this time either, but swinging her head between me and the door, and at my clothes on the floor, too.

'You want me to follow you somewhere?'

She jumps up like she's on a trampoline.

My heart leaps with her. I can't hear Mum up, but what if she wakes up on a Good Morning again, and waits for her hug in the kitchen, and I'm not there to give one?

The fox lets out a noise like a bark, and it's the first time I've ever heard a ghost make a proper noise and it sounds just as they look – echoey and loud, but also stretched into softness, like bad TV reception.

I think the noise surprises us both.

I get dressed into my weekend clothes. My purple dungarees, a T-shirt and my tiger-striped socks. I can see in the mirror that my brown hair is wild and my fringe is all over the place, but I don't brush it as usual and I follow the ghost fox out of my bedroom, and tiptoe across the landing to Mum's bedroom.

Her door is closed, and the lasagne I made for her is still outside with the note, untouched.

I reach out and put my hand on the wood.

Today won't be a Good Morning. I can almost feel the thrum of her angry ghosts behind the door and wish that I could make them go away for her.

The doctors are trying and Mum is trying even harder, but they all say it takes time.

My own ghost barks at me again from halfway down the stairs. I turn and give her a nod, following her.

She watches me as I get my shoes on and runs straight through the front door when I open it.

The new day is just stretching its fingers above the horizon, leaving smears the same colour as the fox's fur on the clouds. It's cold enough to see my own breath, so I stop on the doorstep and put on my coat, as the fox trots across the road to the house opposite mine with garden gnomes all over the front step, and starts barking again, loudly.

My insides drop and I look back to the house for Mum before remembering that no one can see or hear ghost animals but me. And I almost laugh, but then I spot a curtain in the house opposite, twitching.

Hissing to the ghost fox to *be quiet*, I take my bike out of the shed, lock on my helmet and push off into the morning. But I hear the noise of another front door opening, before—

'Nora! Nora Frost!'

I swing my head back and see the camouflage coat of Kwame, clumsily trying to steer his own bike out of the front garden with the gnomes. The ghost fox barks happily, waiting for him to catch up for some reason.

I slam on my brakes. 'Stop shouting,' I hiss. 'You'll wake everyone up.'

He cycles across the road to pull up next to me, his jumper on backwards and his helmet not even done up.

'I saw you from the window – I've been up with my grandad for a whole half-hour already. Where are you going?'

I look at the fox, now trotting happily up the road. Kwame peers with me and I stop to glance at his eyes, unfocused on the place where a rainbow-glittered fox is disappearing onto the cycle path.

'Never mind,' I sigh, pushing off again.

'Hey – wait for me!' I hear him fumbling for his pedals and I ride faster, skidding round onto the path the other side of the treeline and looking for the fox –

somehow now a whole world in the distance, like a star shooting away from me.

'Wait up!' Kwame shouts again from behind me.

'Go back home!' I call over my shoulder. 'I told you – I don't need you.'

I only need my bike with the twelve gears and go-faster red paint. My mum bought it for me for my ninth birthday and it's the best thing I own because it's mine. I pump my feet on the pedals and it feels like I've sprouted wings. My handlebars are slick with dew, and the morning sits still like a picture I'm making

come alive. Cycling makes me feel free – like I can go anywhere and be anything, so I lift my bum off the seat of my bike and pedal fast. The air whips my hair back and squeezes cold in my lungs. And the ghost fox ahead of me zigzags across the path like she's feeling alive, too.

I can still hear Kwame panting behind me and smile when the fox leaps over a hedge towards the canal path. I come this way all the time, so don't slow down to skid between the metal bollards as I race towards the thin path the fox is now running along. I do swing my head back to check on Kwame though and giggle when I see his bike getting caught up in the narrow space between the bollards.

The fox barks again and I whoop with her, cycling faster.

I like it down here. The canal is still and murky with tangled lily pads disappearing into the depths. If you look hard enough, you can see the ripple of a fish or the glint of a drowned shopping trolley. There are also bridges to ride over, which make my stomach flip like I might not come back down the other side, and long tunnels that I call out my name in the middle of and hear it echo back to me.

The path narrows even more, with metal bolts jutting out of the side where boats are sometimes tied. There are no boats here today though – just me and the fox, getting faster and faster ahead.

My legs are pumping on the pedals so fast that it's throwing me left and right. I skid round the bend, throwing up dust under my tyres as the fox turns back to check to see if I'm catching up.

I am.

My breaths are tight and my legs are singing, but I'm almost close enough to the fox now to see the rainbow colours flickering on the edges of her somehow-silent paws, and the sun strangely shining through her body like she's a picture on a stained-glass window.

I feel brave and alive and like I can do anything. I close my eyes for a moment to feel the coldness in my chest thaw like a melting iceberg. But then I open them again, and instead of seeing the ghost fox running ahead of me, she's stopped. Right in the middle of the path. Looking at me.

I wobble and try to catch my handlebars again to brake, but they slip out from under me.

Insides jolting as my foot slaps the path, suddenly I'm rolling, dirt and paving stones biting me, my helmet clattering stars into my eyes. The whole world turns rainbow, and when I finally stop skidding along the ground, I look up to see my bike dropping over the canal edge and sinking into the murky water.

'No!' I shout, scrambling to the edge, reaching over the side and catching the very tip of the handlebars with my fingers before they sink out of sight. I try to pull the bike back up with all my might, but the rubber feels slippery and I don't have a good enough grip.

Suddenly, I hear a skidding behind me and a pair of golden-brown hands plunge into the water, so I can feel fingers sliding over mine.

'I think I've got it!' Kwame says next to me, but he doesn't, because neither do I.

The bike slips down, the weeds at the bottom of the canal pulling and pulling from below. I feel hot and my heart thumps loud in my ears. Somewhere, I hear the ghost fox, barking.

'Get off!' I shout.

'But I have it. If you just move, I can help pull—'

'I don't need your help!'

There's a sharp intake of breath and the hands slip away.

For a moment, my bike stays in my fingertips. For

a moment, I can see myself dragging it back up like sunken treasure.

But then the canal closes its talons round it from the bottom and the handlebars slip from my fingers. And I watch as my brilliant red bike sinks down into the water, out of sight.

6

For what seems for ever and no time at all, I just look at the place my bike disappeared, like it might float back up again and what just happened not be real. But all I can see are bubbles from where the silty canal bottom is claiming it as its own.

'Are you okay?' Kwame asks from behind me.

I snap my head round. He looks sweaty from the cycle ride, his jumper still on backwards.

'You lost my bike,' I say, anger now bubbling up with the pain in my hands and knees from where I fell.

His eyes go wide. 'It was already in the water when I got here.'

It's true, but I don't want it to be, because that means it's my fault that I lost my bike and it's going to upset Mum and make her worse. I feel like crying, so I look away.

'What happened?' he asks. 'You were riding so fast, I thought you were going to follow your bike into the water.'

The ghost fox. I scramble up, wiping my eyes, trying to find a hint of rainbow on the path around us, but there's nothing but an old plastic bag caught on a tree.

'I lost her, too,' I whisper.

Kwame follows my gaze. 'Lost who? I can help you find them if you like. Or I can help you get home. You can ride my bike.'

'I told you, I don't need any help,' I say firmly, taking one last look at the empty water before turning to set off for home. But as soon as I start walking, I feel pain surging up from my ankle and I call out, accidentally clinging onto Kwame's shoulder as he walks me towards a broken bench.

I look down and see the path has cut the knees of my dungarees and my hands are scratched and bleeding. I lift my foot up, expecting to see broken bones, but it just looks normal, so I think it's okay.

I feel broken though. Like I'm the one that slipped into the canal and drowned. All I can see when I close my eyes is Mum's face draining of colour again.

Kwame sits on the edge of the bench away from me. He doesn't say anything and I'm glad, because I don't want to talk either. After a while though, he takes out a battered notebook and starts drawing in it.

I take my helmet off, staring into the water. 'I'm sorry I shouted at you,' I say, quietly.

'I'm sorry you lost your bike,' he says back.

I swallow, feeling that sorry in my chest like a bruise.

I peer over his arm to see what he's drawing. It's a school exercise book, but inside is a rainbow of coloured pencil drawings of mythical creatures and fox-like monsters with bat wings and lion manes.

'What are they?' I ask.

He doesn't look up. 'Just a game I play with my brothers. They all give me animal names and I combine them into something new and powerful.'

He turns the page back to show me elephants with antlers, and at the bottom I see a drawing of a girl with messy hair standing under a weeping cherry tree with a label:

Nora doesn't need any help.

It's a bit weird to see my name and face like that in someone else's workbook, even if the drawing is actually quite good. Kwame is a bit weird in general really, with his backwards jumper and his following me around, even though I've told him a thousand times to go away.

But then, I'm a bit weird too, I suppose. I see ghost animals and heat up my own lasagne and spend all my lunchtimes on my own, so the teachers have sent home notes from school to Mum about it. Once, Mum pulled me onto her lap and said that it's good to be weird. That all the best people are and the trick is to find the people who are the same type of weird as you.

The canal water seems to flicker rainbows.

Kwame scratches his leg and his grey joggers ride up, revealing tiger-striped socks, the same as mine. And I start speaking without really deciding to.

'It was a ghost fox I saw, under the tree.'

Kwame looks up, not even blinking.

'I was following her then too, on my bike – before I fell off. And she sat with me all last night.'

I look over my shoulder to where the fox disappeared, the path empty of rainbow.

I've not told anyone but Mum about the ghost animals – probably because I haven't seen them for a long time. But Mum thought they were just a dream, so I'm expecting Kwame to say something like that too. That they're all in my head. That I've made them up.

That I'm lying.

He frowns for a moment, looking around like maybe I'm playing a trick on him. But then he looks down at his drawings again – of the fox-like creature with the bat wings and the antlers – and he smiles.

He turns to a blank page. 'Did it have wings like a hawk? How big were its fangs?'

I frown. 'It might be a ghost, but it's still just a fox.'

'Oh,' he says disappointedly, before shrugging. 'That's not normally how we play, but that's still cool. Does it float in the air? Can you see through it?'

'You believe me?'

He's already drawing, bent over his notebook with

his tongue out. 'Huh? Oh – yeah. Ghost fox – does it have any superpowers?'

I stare at him. He's still wearing his helmet and it makes his head look really big. But his eyes are kind and filled with something else too – excitement. And it kick-starts my cold heart racing again.

'She doesn't float or have powers, but she has rainbow edges. They flicker – like TV static. And I think she understands me . . .'

Kwame nods, writing this all down in his book around the drawing. 'Is she alone, or are there more?'

The word 'alone' makes my insides squeeze. I look round for her again. 'She's on her own . . . but she's gone now.'

Kwame stands up to look. 'My grandad took me to see a fox den in the old scrapyard last year. Maybe we should go on our own Fox Hunt now. And – oh – maybe she'll have friends too, like a dragon, or a—'

I sigh loudly and roll my eyes until he grins.

'Come on, Nora; it'll be fun.'

I look down at my ankle and he picks up his bike.

'You can ride behind me on the seat. I'm always giving backies to my brothers; it's easy.'

I bite my lip, thinking about the drawing of the girl

under the tree he did with the line, *Nora doesn't need any help.*

'Come on,' he says again. 'I promise not to help you in any way. And if I go home now, I'll only have to babysit my brothers, so you'll actually really be helping *me* out.'

I stand up slowly, clipping on my helmet.

He grins, his dimple-craters back as he gives me space to climb onto the back of his bike, being careful not to put too much weight on my still-sore ankle.

'This,' he says, 'is going to be brilliant, Nora Frost.'

7

Kwame might be good at drawing, but he's rubbish at riding a bike.

He's really slow, which is fine when we're on the canal path, as he's also wobbly and I really don't want to end up in the murky water with my bike. But once we get up the bank and onto the dirt path leading towards the old scrapyard, it starts to get a bit boring and bumpy. There are sticks on the path that crack under our tyres and thorns that reach out their fingers to us as we pass. And even when we get to the hill that leads us down towards the valley the scrapyard sits in, he puts on his brakes so we squeal carefully down.

'Can't you go any faster?' I say in his ear.

He laughs. 'Sometimes it's nicer to go slowly. It means you don't miss anything.'

I sigh, but look around anyway. The sun is all the way up now and is shooting bars of light through the canopy of leaves above us. I can hear the creak of a woodpecker hammering on a tree somewhere and smell the brambles that line the path. It is nice, and seeing it helps heal the hurt of losing my bike. But I don't tell Kwame that.

When we get to the bottom, we see the sign for the old scrapyard and towers of old cars, fridges and claws of metal behind a chain fence that someone has knocked down. I remember coming here with Saffie and her dad once, when the scrapyard was run by an old lady with no teeth, and she helped Saffie's dad get a replacement seat for his car. But no one runs the scrapyard now, and the crushed cars feel spooky, like a broken graveyard.

Kwame stops the bike and climbs off it. 'It's cool here, isn't it? My dad doesn't like me coming without adult supervision, but we'll be careful. How's your ankle?'

He tries to hold my hand as I swing my leg off, but I pull it away. I try putting weight on both feet, testing them out for twists of pain.

'Better, I think,' I say. 'Where did you say you saw the fox den?'

'Around the other side – my grandad says this is the perfect place for a Fox Hunt, as foxes love it here. There must be loads of rats hiding in the junk for them to eat. I drew a picture of a fox-rat actually – want to see?'

I throw my helmet on the floor with Kwame's bike and walk over the broken fence where he pointed, ignoring his question. He scuttles after me.

The scrapyard stretches as wide and as high as we can see, with towering walls of broken things. Some of the cars have been squeezed into mangled bricks, whilst others have their roofs peeled off like cans of sardines. It smells sharp, like nettles and animals, and I keep my eye out for glimpses of rainbow.

'Nora! Come and look at this,' Kwame says, climbing up the back of a rusty crane that's balanced on the top of a big mound of mud. He opens a door and climbs into a seat at the front, where giant levers once controlled a huge hook at the top to lift cars on top of each other.

'That's not being careful,' I say, frowning.

My mum used to tell me stories of people she'd helped on building sites who had played around with machinery like this. *'It's all fun and games until someone gets hurt,'* she'd said.

I walk away, Kwame laughing happily and pretending to shoot things using the buttons and levers inside, chattering excitedly to himself about aliens. I jog round the corner and stop dead because there – standing on a microwave that's half drowned in a puddle of mud – is the ghost fox.

I look behind me to call Kwame, but then stop myself. I found her without him. I bend down quietly so he can't see where I am and put my hand out to her again.

'I didn't run you over with my bike.'

The ghost fox doesn't put her head into my hand this time, but starts barking again at me, making me jump back to my feet.

'What?' I say, stepping away from her teeth as she snaps close to my ankles.

She runs round me, stalking close to the ground behind me as if she's hunting for something. I follow her, crouching low to look back round the corner to Kwame's crane, when I hear a voice, shouting.

'Hey, look – it's Barmy Kwame.'

I squint through the rainbow aura of the ghost fox and see Joel swaggering up the mound of mud to the crane with a rusty pole in his hand. Kwame meanwhile fumbles for the handle to the door, his head so far down, his chin is practically on his chest.

Joel hops up and kicks the door closed, so Kwame is trapped inside again. 'What you doing in my grandma's old scrapyard all alone?'

Kwame looks like he wants to disappear. He mumbles something I can't hear and Joel laughs.

'Ohhh, you're playing out with all your imaginary friends!' He pretends to bow to an invisible person to his left, putting on a posh voice. '*How do you* do, *imaginary person.*'

'But you're here alone,' Kwame mutters.

Joel's smile falls away. Kwame quickly goes for the door handle again, but Joel raises the pole he's holding high, before jamming it down into the handle from the other side. He sneers.

'How about we play a real game, Barmy?'

'No thanks,' I hear Kwame say, quietly.

'Ohhh, come on, it's fun. It's called Runaway Crane.' Joel jumps off the crane, landing with his knees bent. 'You're in the crane . . .' He goes round the back and starts kicking at the wheel chocks that are stopping the crane from slipping down the mound of mud it's balanced on. 'And I'll make it run away . . .' He kicks the chocks again until one comes loose, making the crane tip dangerously, and Kwame shouts out.

The ghost fox growls and so do I.

'Hey!' I say, standing up, my fists clenched. 'Step off!'

Joel spins round, fear flitting across his face for a moment until he spots me and sneers instead.

'Who's this, Kwame? Your girlfriend?'

'I'm his friend. And what you're doing is really dangerous, Joel.'

The ghost fox barks at my feet, but Joel can't see or hear her, so he just laughs.

'I know,' he says. 'That's the point.'

He gives the other wheel chock a huge kick and the crane groans loudly like a sinking ship, making Kwame shout out loud again and the smile fall right off Joel's face.

'No!' I yell, running forward as Joel steps back.

The crane slowly starts sliding down the mound, turning dangerously, throwing Kwame around inside the cabin with his eyes wide. At the bottom, twists of metal spikes jut out of the ground, with scraps of

50

metal littered all the way down.

Jumping up onto the side of the crane, I try with all my might to take the pole out of the handle as Kwame hammers on the glass door. But Joel has shoved it in really tightly.

I spin round, looking for Joel and see him disappearing round the corner, tripping over his feet in his desperation to get away.

'I'm trapped!' Kwame shouts.

I'm scared and angry at Joel for leaving as the crane starts to pick up speed down the hill. I look around for the ghost fox to make me feel stronger, but she's disappeared, too.

Just then, the crane hits the broken door of an old bus, jolting me off the side and onto my back on the ground. And I close my eyes, expecting the crane to flip over with Kwame inside, when the creaking noise stops.

The crane has come to a standstill. I get to my feet carefully, opening my eyes to look for Kwame in the cabin, but he's nowhere to be seen.

'Kwame?' I say, my voice shaking.

'Yes?' Kwame says from behind me, dusting himself off.

I lurch on the spot and see him – alive and still

wearing his helmet and his backwards jumper and his coat. I give him a huge hug, which surprises us both.

'How did you . . . ?' I look to the crane, with the pole still shoved in the door handle.

'Oh,' Kwame says, sheepishly. 'There was another door.'

I flick his arm, but laugh, and he laughs with me. We both collapse onto the ground on our backs, looking at the towers of cars touching the sky around us.

'Are you okay?' he asks.

I nod, wiping my hands on my dungarees. 'That was scary.'

Kwame laughs again. 'You should try being in a runaway crane!'

I frown, sitting up and looking at him. 'Why do you let him treat you like that?'

He sits up with me, but keeps his head down. 'If I ignore him, then he sometimes goes away.'

'He's a bully,' I say. 'And bullies only respond to strength. Have you told a teacher?'

He shakes his head. 'It's okay, honestly. I'm handling it *fine* on my own.'

I sigh. 'I'm not sure you are.' I put my hand on his shoulder. 'It's a good job I'm here, Kwame.'

He smiles shyly. 'As my friend?'

I drop my hand. But out the corner of my eye, I see the ghost fox standing on the top of the crane and seeing into that cold part of me where my secrets are kept. And I understand now what she was trying to tell me – that maybe being alone all the time isn't very helpful.

I roll my eyes, but smile. 'Yeah, okay. As your friend.'

He smiles, writing something down in his notebook under the picture of me. I catch a glimpse and it's just four words, with the last one underlined three times.

Nora is my friend.

PART TWO

THE HARE

8

By the time Kwame has ridden us all the way back home, my stomach is rumbling like thunder.

He rides into the drive opposite my house, where several garden gnomes seem to be having a party on the front step.

'You said your grandad lives here?' I ask.

Kwame unclips his helmet and nods his head. 'Yeah. I live round the corner with my mum and dad and four brothers. Things are really busy there all the time though, so I come here to stay with Grandad a lot.'

I whistle. 'Four brothers is a lot of boys.'

Kwame wrinkles his nose. 'Yeah, our house pretty much always smells of feet.'

I laugh, looking across the road to the red front door of my own house. It doesn't smell of feet. It used to smell of soap and baking and DIY. And it still does sometimes. But now there's a new smell – a sticky, hot smell, like when you're sick and spend all day in bed.

'Do you want to come in for some food?' Kwame asks. 'I can make us a sandwich – my grandad has enough pickle in the cupboard to feed a whole country.'

I can feel his eyes on me, so I shake my head. 'Thanks, but my mum is making a big dinner later,' I lie.

I walk slowly across the road.

'See you later?' Kwame shouts.

'Yeah,' I say, waving but not looking.

I get to the front door and I'm not sure about going in, because there's no note this time. And this part is always nice and not nice, because Mum could be inside making fairy cakes, or she could still be locked in her bedroom.

I can feel Kwame watching me again, so I dig my keys out of my back pocket and open the door, almost knocking straight into Mum. Her hair is up in a messy bun and her eyes are wide and scared.

'Nora!' she shouts, pulling me inside. 'Where have you—?'

But then she looks down and sees my torn dungarees and my scratched-up hands and the mud, and her face crumbles.

'What happened?!'

'Sorry,' I say quickly, my insides twisting. 'I was cycling by the canal. And I fell off and—'

Mum hugs me to her and then quickly lets me go again, her face pale and angry. 'I wake up and you're gone – no note. And then you come home looking like this! I thought something terrible had happened!' she shouts, and I put my head down, all the heat rising up into my cheeks.

'I'm sorry. It was an accident.'

But Mum's not listening. Her voice is shaking and she's worried and I did that and the sorry feels like a ball of white-hot lava in my chest.

I squeeze my eyes closed as she shouts, trying not to cry. And I try to remember what the doctor said to me – that sometimes Mum might get angry. That it's her PTSD and not me. But I can't remember what to do to make it better again.

'Look at me when I'm talking to you, young lady.'

I lift my head up, but my glasses have fogged up, so I just see Mum's angry shape in a haze and a frightened flit of rainbow jumping from the stairs behind her.

I freeze and Mum stops shouting too, turning to look with me.

'What?' she says, shakily.

I squint, looking for hints of the fox, but I don't see her. Mum turns back to me. Her hands are shaking, so I quickly take them in mine.

'It's nothing. I'm sorry – I didn't mean to fall. And I lost my bike in the canal and it's gone and now you're angry and I – I can't remember how to make it better, Mum. I'm sorry . . .'

My crying gets worse, even though I'm really trying to stop. And behind Mum I see flashes of long rainbow-tinged ears running frantically round the hall with my thoughts. I can't see it properly, but it isn't a ghost fox. It's something else, and it's frightened.

Mum rubs her face and takes a deep breath, like she's trying to pull something huge from deep inside her.

'Oh, Nora, I'm sorry. It's – my symptoms are really playing up today.' She puts her hand on my shoulder, squeezing it tight. 'I spent all that time in bed with my thoughts yesterday and then seeing you all banged up like this . . .' She takes another deep breath and folds me into a huge hug, which only makes me cry harder.

'I'm sorry for making it worse, Mum,' I say.

She kisses my head over and over, saying, 'It's not your fault, remember?'

She helps me take my shoes off and leads me into the living room, pulling back the curtains and letting the light in. Then she sits next to me on the sofa, brushing back my hair and looking at me right in the eye.

She looks tired, and I wonder if my accident made that worse.

'I'm sorry for shouting, sweetheart.'

'I'm sorry for losing my bike, Mum.'

She pulls me into another hug, talking into my hair about how it's a shame about the bike, but she only cares about me being okay. And I only care about her, too and I'm *sorry*.

My glasses get fogged up again, so I take them off as Mum heaves herself up to fetch the first-aid kit from the kitchen cupboard.

The living room is quiet without her. I clean my glasses on my T-shirt and try to remind myself that everything is *fine* when I spot the running rainbow again. I squint as it leaps from the mantel to the chair to the coffee table.

I put my glasses back on quickly. She looks like a long rabbit, with gangly legs and ragged fur. A hare, I think.

A *ghost* hare.

I jolt to my feet just as Mum opens the door and the hare takes off running through it.

'Come on, off with those muddy clothes,' Mum says, not noticing my craning neck.

Both our hands are still shaking, so we work together to undo the fastening on my dungarees. As she cleans the scratches on my knees and palms though, her hands get steadier and her breathing returns to normal.

'It's nice seeing you fix people again,' I say, quietly.

She smiles slightly before frowning, putting a plaster over my cuts. 'I'd rather not have to fix you though.' She looks at me, seriously. 'You need to take better care, Nora. Promise me you'll be sensible and stay safe?'

I sit up tall. 'I will – you don't have to worry about me.'

Mum used to tell me stories about the people she'd helped from her ambulance. She's been there for babies and old people and everyone in between. Sometimes, she'd help so many people in one day that she'd come

62

home with no more help to give herself.

I wonder if she's remembering those times, as a small crease appears on her forehead and I quickly stand up.

'I feel much better now,' I say. 'Let's go outside somewhere.'

Mum looks out at the sun and bites her lip. 'Nora . . .'

But then my stomach rumbles loudly and Mum laughs, loud. It sounds like bells.

'I've got a better idea. How about you go have a wash and put some clean clothes on and I'll make us some soup with hot bread? How does that sound?'

My stomach rumbles again and she kisses my head, packing all the plasters back in a box and shoving them at the very back of the cupboard.

After my shower, I look everywhere in my room for the ghost hare. I don't find her, so maybe she escaped. I hope if she did, she's less frightened now.

When I get down to the kitchen, Mum is still staring at the back of a carton of soup, trying to blink in the words.

'Here, let me,' I say, tipping it out into a microwave

bowl and setting the timer. 'Why don't you check on the bread?'

Mum kisses my head. 'What would I do without you, hey?' she says, making my insides feel warm like they're already full of soup.

Mum opens the oven and tips a cooked loaf of part-baked bread that we've had in the cupboard for ages onto a plate. She sighs in the smell and goes to touch the top, but I bat her hand away.

'It's too hot!'

She laughs. 'Who's the mum here?'

Mum ladles the soup into bowls. She gathers it all onto a tray, but instead of putting everything on the table where yesterday morning's flowers are already starting to droop, she carries it into the living room.

We sit cuddled on the sofa under a blanket together. Mum butters me some bread and we dip it into our bowls and it's like a hug on the inside. It's starting to feel like a Good Afternoon, so I turn to her to ask if we can watch some of our favourite Disney films, when I see she's fallen asleep.

I watch her for a bit – her forehead creased like she's having a nightmare. And I feel the twist of guilt come back from having made her so worried before.

I cover her with all of the blanket and turn on the TV to watch Disney with the sound down, singing to all our favourite songs under my breath. Slowly, I inch towards her, until my head is resting on her chest and I can feel her heart beating in time to the music.

When the credits roll, the hare hops in through the living-room door again, freezing when she spots us cuddled on the sofa.

'Hello,' I whisper. 'Have you come to be my friend, too?'

Her ears prick up and I can see her rainbow heart beating so fast, it makes her ribs quiver.

'It's okay,' I whisper. 'There's nothing to be afraid of.'

The hare looks between me and Mum, jumping back up on the coffee table, and I smile at her. I try to move away from Mum slowly so I don't wake her up, and I stretch my hand out towards the hare's twitching nose.

My fingers get closer and closer, until they're almost touching her rainbow-flicking fur. 'See,' I whisper. 'Everything is *fine*.'

But then Mum shifts in her sleep, making me jump because I'm worried that my words have woken her. And the hare startles too, her ears flattening and her long legs jumping off the table.

I want to jump up and follow her too, maybe over to Kwame's grandad's house, where there are pickle sandwiches. But Mum sighs, the crease returning to her forehead as she goes back to sleep, and I watch my maybe friend the hare run out of the door without me.

9

I don't wake up on Sunday until the sun is already shining bright. I scramble for my glasses, looking around for traces of fox or hare, but finding no rainbows anywhere.

My heart sinks. Even though the fox made me run into a bully, sink my bike and almost lose Kwame in a scrapyard yesterday, it was still nice having her around. The ghost animals have always made me feel brave. And the fox made me feel less alone somehow – maybe because she forced me to make friends with Kwame, who turned out to be my kind of weird. The hare I saw yesterday seemed different to the fox and I wonder what it is she wants. She might need my help.

I climb out of bed and pull back my curtains, squinting at the street. My bedroom is at the front of the house, so I can see the entrance to the cycle path I follow on the way to school, and the street winding down the hill. I look and look, but there's no sign of any rainbow glints, sneaking round the corner.

I'm about to give up and see if Mum has woken up yet, when I notice the curtain across the road, twitching. Kwame's face appears, his smile lighting up the whole window of his grandad's house.

He waves and I give a small wave back. He's trying to say something, but even with my glasses on, I can't make out what it is. I mime a big shrug at him and he beckons me over.

I step back from the curtains and listen. There's no movement in the bedroom next to mine.

I look back at Kwame. I'm not sure how to mime *I might come over, but it depends if this is a Good Morning or not.* So I just hold up a finger like *I'll just be one minute* and his smile beams back.

I get dressed and tiptoe across the landing to Mum's closed door. I can't hear anything on the other side, so I walk quietly down the stairs, checking the empty rooms for Mum or a glimmer of ghost, not finding anything but a bunch of old photos all over the kitchen table and a pile of dirty dishes.

I pour myself some cereal, looking at the old photos of me from when I was a baby. Mum always says I looked just like my dad when I was small, but I think I look the most like her. We have the same pointy chin, stick-out ears and wild brown hair. But my hair was a lot lighter back then, and when I see pictures of me and Dad together, it almost looks like he's cut off some of his hair to stick on my head.

In the pictures, Dad is taking me exploring up hills, along beaches and in caves – both of us wearing his trademark tiger stripes on our hats and T-shirts. I still like to wear tiger stripes now, partly to show that I'm a wonderfully weird and wild thing like Dad, and partly because they remind me of the ghost tiger that sat with me and made me feel strong after he left. But I only wear the stripes on my socks now, as sometimes Mum can get sad when she's reminded about their divorce. It's *fine* being just me and her, and it's not like Dad doesn't call. He's just doing important work, he says, saving wildcats in India.

As I flick through the photos, I notice a shadowy figure standing in the background of a lot of them. At first, I think it's Mum – but this person is taller and stands straighter than she does, arms crossed over their chest. I'm squinting at one of the photos, trying to work out what the shape is sitting on their shoulder, when a knock comes at the front door.

I leap up, running to the door to open it before even more noise wakes Mum up, and find Kwame on the doorstep.

'You said you'd just be a minute!' he says too loudly.

'Shh,' I hiss, grabbing my keys and shoes and closing the door.

He doesn't listen though, scurrying across the road, so I have to jog to catch up. And when we get to his grandad's house, he almost makes me kick over the gnomes on the front step as he pulls me through the door and tries to take my shoes off, which is a strange and impossible thing to do when I'm standing up in them. I kick him off and do it myself.

'Come on!' he says, beckoning me to follow him through the house, which does smell a bit like pickle.

The walls are lined with photos in brown frames and the kitchen is a mishmash of different-coloured furniture, like it's been pieced together from a whole street of other people's kitchens.

Outside the window, a garden stretches much further than ours at home does, and I can see blurry shapes of boys rocketing round it.

'Who are they?' I ask as Kwame pushes the back door open and their shouting gets louder.

Kwame rolls his eyes. 'My brothers. Owen is the one wearing the bin-bag cape, Payne is the one chasing him, and baby John is probably eating grass somewhere. Ignore them – they're not normally here.'

I follow him into the tangle of a back garden behind the house, our matching tiger-striped socks hopping across the stepping stones.

Owen and Payne almost run into us, and I notice that they look like Kwame, but in a strange not-quite way. Owen has Kwame's same Afro haircut, but his face is longer and his eyebrows thicker. Payne also has Kwame's wide eyes, but his dimple is in his chin, not his cheeks. They shoot at each other with invisible guns, shouting and pushing, and I have to sidestep baby John, who is pulling grass out of the lawn with a devilish grin.

Kwame puts his head down, ignoring them, leading me to an old caravan parked at the bottom. Everywhere is wild weeds and clawing ivy and insects buzzing. Even the caravan has green-tinged edges and broken wheels and windows, like the garden is clutching it to its heart.

'It feels like we're in a jungle!' I shout over the arguing brothers behind us.

Kwame roars like his tiger-striped socks are his real skin and swings the door to the caravan open.

Only it's not just a caravan. The whole inside is filled with dozens of pictures of the same rainbow ghost fox.

10

I gasp, putting my arm out to stop Kwame bustling into the caravan.

'What is this?' I whisper.

Kwame beams, ducking under my arm. 'Do you like them? I spent all yesterday afternoon drawing them – I almost went through a whole pack of pencils.'

He slams the door behind us, wobbling a bookcase that looks like it's about to fall down. In fact, everything looks like it's about to fall down in the caravan. There are two worn armchairs next to a hole in the wall,

where I can see weeds poking through. There's a kitchen worktop piled high with dirty plant pots; a rickety table and chairs near the broken window. And it's all covered in drawings of my ghost fox.

I pick one up from the table. It looks like her – with the same black-tip ears and hungry jaws.

'I've never drawn a fox that was just a fox before – even though it's a rainbow one. Usually, I draw them with fangs or manes or something. I thought it might be a bit boring, but foxes are actually quite cool, don't you think? I looked them up with my grandad – apparently they have whiskers on their face and legs too, and they eat berries as well as animals and stuff.'

He's speaking fast, shifting from foot to foot and avoiding my eye. I grab his arm, looking at him to make him stop.

'They're perfect, Kwame. They look just like her.'

Kwame beams, flopping onto the worn chairs with me so the broken springs jut up into our backs. He takes out his exercise book and tips his pencils out onto the floor.

'What shall I draw next? Maybe a kangaroo, or – oh – an eagle would be cool.'

I grip the sides of the armchair, looking back towards the caravan door. 'What about a hare?'

Kwame scrunches his nose. 'Like a rabbit?'

Just then, the caravan door swings open and an old man with a walking stick laughs, shaking his head.

'Kwame – hares are completely different animals to rabbits! It's like you don't listen to a word your old grandad says.'

The old man lifts a slippered foot onto the step and Kwame leaps off the chair, helping his grandad into the caravan and onto his chair. I fidget in the one next to him, not sure what I should do, until Kwame flops down next to me, practically sitting on my lap. I give him a kick.

'What's the difference, then?' Kwame asks, wriggling away from me.

Kwame's grandad smiles, dimples like the ones Kwame has just about visible on his wrinkled face. His hair has receded on his head and is the same wispy white as his eyebrows and goatee.

'Hares are much bigger. They have longer ears, tails, and are the fastest land animals in the whole of the UK.'

'Are they really?' I ask as Kwame writes all this down.

'They can go at forty-five miles an hour when they want to!' the old man says. 'And how fast can you go, Miss . . . ?'

Kwame scribbles something on a clean page, ripping it out and tucking it into the pocket of my T-shirt, so it sticks out.

Nora Frost —

Kwame's friend.

It feels like a badge, and the old man smiles when he reads it.

'For my memory,' he says to me. 'Kwame's a good lad, always helping.'

Kwame nods, starting to draw a pair of long ears in his book. 'Nora's really fast on a bike, Grandad. She could probably go forty-five miles an hour if she wanted to.'

The old man beams. 'Oh, I'd love to see that. Can you show me, Nora?'

I can feel myself blushing. 'Yeah, if I still had my bike.'

'I bet you're fast at running too,' Kwame says, still drawing.

I shrug as the door to the caravan bursts open and Owen and Payne fall inside, out of breath.

'Bet you can't beat me,' Owen says.

Payne pushes him down. 'No way, I'm faster.'

'Stop spying on us!' Kwame says, too quietly for them to hear over their squabbling.

The old man holds up his finger and everyone stops to listen. 'A Hare Race.'

The boys whoop and even Kwame jumps up to charge outside, leaving me and the old man together on the chairs.

He looks at me. 'Nora? You don't want to play?'

I pick at the broken fabric. 'I'm too old for games like that.'

He narrows his eyes. 'And I suppose you want to find your ghost hare, don't you?'

My heart skips and I dart an angry look outside to where Kwame is following after his brothers. 'He told you?'

Kwame's grandad laughs. 'Oh, don't worry – I saw his notes and drawings. My memory might not be what it was, but I've always found that a lot can be gained from a little light reading.'

I sigh and look at the old man from the corner of my eye, wondering if he believes me. 'The hare keeps running away – I'm not sure what she wants.'

He shifts on his chair as the boys shout from outside. 'I spent a lot of my youth tracking animals in this caravan all across Europe, you know. Hares are especially tricky as they're very fast, but also extraordinarily good at hiding. They'll freeze when they're frightened, which makes them difficult to spot. You might struggle to find your hare.'

I look outside the broken window to where Kwame is watching his brothers race round the garden.

'Kwame's good at hiding and I found him.'

The old man blinks. 'That's very perceptive, Nora.' He looks at me, hard. 'And what about you? Do you hide? Or perhaps you use that speed of yours to run away from your problems?'

Out of the window, I spot the flash of a rainbow, running at the heels of one of Kwame's brothers.

I leap up into the air, my blood whooshing in my ears. The rainbow disappears.

'I'm not running away,' I say firmly.

Kwame's grandad nods at me, his smile revealing more gaps in his teeth, and I try to step outside the caravan slowly, even though my legs are itching to chase the hare.

Outside, I blink at the sun and the weeds and Kwame's brothers running round the path. One of them leaps high into the air, landing like a superhero on the grass, before looking at the piece of paper tucked into my T-shirt and freezing.

'Nora is the hare!' the boy shouts, pointing.

I hear a yell and Kwame's other brother comes charging out of the bushes, holding the toddler I saw picking grass before. They both try to grab the paper, but I duck, weaving between their outstretched arms.

'What are you doing?' I snap, looking around for the ghost hare.

'The paper in your T-shirt, Nora – that makes you the hare,' Kwame says, as he leaps in front of me, hands curled like claws. 'And we're the hounds, coming to get it.'

Kwame lunges for me, but I spin round, hopping over a row of tangled flower beds. All the boys shout and I dart off, zigzagging along the path so they can't catch me. Kwame tries to corner me, but I spot what he's doing and slide under his legs, so his eyebrows disappear into his hair.

The boys laugh and I'm surprised to hear that I'm laughing, too.

'She's too good!' one of Kwame's brothers says.

His grandad stands in the window of the caravan, clapping his hands, and his words from before canter into my head – maybe I'm fast because I'm good at running away from my problems.

I grind to a halt close to the house, Kwame almost banging into me before he manages to finally snatch the paper from my T-shirt.

'I got it! I got—' he shouts, before one of his brothers immediately snatches it back and runs off, the other one chasing him. 'Oh.'

He smiles breathlessly though, lying down on the grass and taking his notebook from his pocket. 'That was fun.'

I sit down next to him, picking daisies out the lawn. I keep thinking about what Kwame's grandad said about me running away from my problems and it's making my bones tingle with angry thoughts. 'Your grandad thinks he knows a lot, doesn't he?' I mutter.

Kwame frowns slightly. 'He *does* know a lot. He was a scientist before he retired. His memory is going a bit and he gets me and my brothers confused all the time, but he knows loads about animals.' He smiles at me. 'Useful for ghost-animal hunting.'

I drop the daisies. 'So, you come here a lot?'

Kwame nods. 'Yeah, all the time. It's quiet here – well, usually.' He stops and gestures to his brothers leaping and shouting at the far end of the garden. 'Also, Grandad needs a bit more help these days with things, although he's rubbish at asking for it.' He looks at me like he's reading me again, and I avoid his eye. 'Some people aren't very good at asking for things like that.'

I clear my throat. 'Do you find it hard sometimes, looking after him?'

I hear the shuffle of his pencil as he draws. 'Sometimes. He can get annoyed at not being able to do the same things he used to and that makes me sad. But you know – my mum and dad also come over all the time and help out, so it's not just me on my own.'

I pick at my hand plasters and the silence stretches.

'Do you have any grandparents?' he asks.

I shake my head. 'My mum's parents died before I was born.'

'And what about your dad's?'

I frown, the shadowy figure from the back of the photographs on the kitchen table flashing into my mind. 'I don't know . . .'

Kwame slaps a perfect drawing of a ghost hare in front of me, its face pointed to the moon. 'Well, you can share my grandad, then. And my mum and dad too, if you like.'

I stand up. 'Thanks, but I've got my own mum, and she's brilliant.'

Kwame is saying things, but I'm not really listening. Before I leave though, I catch sight of his grandad watching me from the caravan and the dark tail of a rainbow hare running from the boys as fast as it can.

II

It's Monday morning, but I wake up to voices coming from downstairs.

Before Mum got PTSD, she'd invite people over all the time and I did too, so our house was always full of people that didn't live here. But it's not been like that for ages now and the new sound makes my heart skip.

I don't bother getting dressed to tiptoe downstairs. When I get to the bottom step though, I notice a pair of big black boots next to my muddy trainers, and a huge coat on the hook that doesn't belong to me or my mum.

I can hear murmurs through the kitchen door now.

'. . . we're managing fine, Bill. Both of us. We don't need any help.'

I sigh in relief when I hear Bill's name and jump the last step to barge into the kitchen, where Mum and Bill are sitting at the table, holding mugs of tea.

Mum stops talking and Bill grins when he sees me, standing to give me a huge hug. 'Nora the explorer! How are you?'

I wrap my arms round his waist. My arms can't reach all the way, but he could hug me twice if he wanted to. He has a thick moustache like a cartoon character, which he likes to play with, and a big, booming voice.

Bill works with my mum as an emergency medical technician. They take it in turns to drive the ambulance, with one of them in front and the other one attending to the patient in the back. Mum says they've been through thick and thin together for six years, which makes Bill like a member of our family.

I always thought that if my dad had stuck around to get to know me better, I'd have liked him to be like Bill. But Bill has his own family – two grown-up girls I only ever meet at barbecues.

'What are you doing here?' I say, sitting next to him

on the bench and grabbing some toast.

He laughs. 'Oh, that's charming, that!'

I roll my eyes. 'You know what I mean. I've missed you.'

Bill shoots a look at Mum, who goes red for some reason. I frown, but Bill smiles wide. 'I've missed you too, kiddo. So tell me all about your adventures, then – what's this I hear about a lost bike?' He pokes at one of the now-peeling plasters on my hands.

I blush and tell him about my accident with my eyes avoiding Mum's, being careful not to mention the ghost fox.

'Well, it's a good job you didn't go in that water after it! The amount of times we've been called to that canal, hey, Miri?'

I shoot a look at Mum, because sometimes talking about her job is enough to bring her symptoms on, but she just laughs. 'I felt like we lived there last year – I blame that scout hut with the faulty canoes!'

Bill fills up all our glasses with orange juice and makes even more toast, so we don't have to move. And it feels nice to see Mum laughing at Bill's bad jokes and even nicer when he starts doing the washing-up.

Bill whistles as he pours half the washing-up liquid

into the bowl, so the bubbles grow up like trees, and Mum winks at me.

'What are we doing today?' I ask. 'Is Bill taking us somewhere?'

Bill has a jeep that can go across fields and up hills, so days out with him have always been full of mud and wild things.

Mum smiles, taking a sip of tea. 'You have school, remember?'

'Oh,' I say, grimacing at missing yet another Good Morning. 'Why is Bill here, then?'

Mum looks at Bill's back and lowers her voice to me. 'We have some catching up to do. I tell you what though, if you get ready quickly and ask nicely, maybe Bill can give you a ride to school in the jeep.'

Bill sprays soapy water across the room and I jump up, torn between running upstairs and spending more time with Mum. But she sighs and grabs a tea towel.

'Honestly, Bill, you've got enough suds here to wash an elephant.'

His laugh booms. 'Have you seen your dirty dishes? We need all the help we can get.'

I smile and leave them flicking bubbles at each other at the sink. Upstairs, I wash and change the plasters on my knees and hands, putting another dollop of antiseptic cream on each. The cream is cold and I wince as it stings the cuts, remembering Mum's face when she saw that I'd hurt myself, when suddenly I see the hare leaping out of the bathtub.

We both freeze.

The hare looks the same as Kwame's drawings, with long ears and limbs and a frightened expression.

'You're not running away from me this time,' I whisper.

She keeps looking at me, so I pull on my school uniform. I want to put my hand out and see if I can touch her – to see if she feels like the same cold-emptiness as the fox. But something tells me that trying to touch this ghost animal would just scare her away again, and I don't want that.

I watch for a while, until Mum calls my name from downstairs. 'Nora! You're going to be late!'

The hare's ears twitch and she hops round the bathroom door. I scramble up, racing down the stairs after her. The hare runs for a moment in a circle round my shoes in the hall, before leaping between my legs, so I spin round straight into Bill, who has wet hair and a soggy tea towel on his shoulder.

'Oh!' I shout, as he squeezes me in a one-armed hug,

bending down so his knees crackle.

'Your mum says you'd like a lift in the jeep.'

I nod, trying to see over his head to where the ghost hare might be, my blood fizzing. 'Yeah, please. If that's okay.'

Bill's eyes twinkle. 'Of course.'

I go to step round him – so I can find my ghost hare – but Bill holds my arm, looking in my eyes the same way as Kwame does, as if I'm being read like a book.

'And you're holding up okay, are you? You and your mum?'

My insides get quiet. The hare sneaks round Bill's legs, ears flat. 'We're *fine* thanks, never better.'

'Only your mum was just saying about you cooking your own lasagne the other night and I thought—'

'Oh – I do that all the time; I'm good at it.'

Bill pats my hand. 'That's great. But you know you don't have to do that for your mum, don't you? You know that if you ever need help—'

The hare's ears prick up again, so they're standing tall, but I don't want to listen.

'Actually,' I say, wriggling out of his huge hands, 'I don't need a lift. I forgot that I'm riding to school with my friend Kwame.'

'Oh,' says Bill, standing. 'But, Nora—'

I stamp my shoes on and pick up my school bag, avoiding his eye. 'Thanks for breakfast though. And for the offer. See you soon, I hope!'

I don't look back at Bill or the ghost hare as I take off into the morning. I hardly even stop to look as I run down the road – my watch telling me that I'm going to be late without my bike or a jeep to take me. I try to flatten my thoughts and think only about running forty-five miles per hour and how just because I'm running – just because I'm fast – it doesn't mean that I'm running away from my problems.

I don't even have any problems to run away from, anyway.

I'm *fine*.

12

I watch the seconds *tick*, *tick*, *tick* to Monday afternoon Health and Fitness break, so I can escape the warm classroom out into the cold grey day again. I'm still thinking about coming in late and out of breath this morning, Miss Omar looking at the clock and sighing as she gave me a red late slip – my third one this month, which means a letter home.

All my class watched me as I sat down in my seat, whispering behind their hands.

When 2.15 p.m. finally comes, the cold dampness

outside feels good. Foggy patches hang round the end of the playground, making it look like the edges have been rubbed out.

I'm supposed to be running round getting fit with the rest of the children in my year, but instead I run towards Kwame's weeping cherry tree, diving into the branches and spinning, looking for Kwame – but he's not here. I squat down for a while, my thoughts running in circles, tangling over what Bill and Kwame's grandad said. It's too quiet in here, and so when I hear a shout from outside the cocoon of the tree, I'm almost glad to race out of it.

On the playground, Kwame is speaking shyly to a few people in my class – a piece of paper tucked into his shirt. I bite my lip, thinking he's being bullied again, but when I run over, I find him explaining what a Hare Race is to Saffie and Rachael.

' . . . and then you try and snatch the paper out. It's simple, really.'

'But why is it called a Hare Race?' Saffie asks, not looking sure.

'Because hares have to be fast to survive,' I say, snatching the paper out of Kwame's shirt and tucking it into my own. 'Like me.'

Kwame beams and Saffie shouts, chasing me round the playground. Others see what we're doing and join in – a boy from Kwame's class manages to corner me and snatch the paper from me near the tadpole pond. Kwame runs at my heels as he chases him, his smile wider than I've ever seen it. Soon, it feels like the whole year is playing Kwame's game, and I don't think it even matters to Kwame that he's not fast enough to catch the hare. It's his game and he's running – not hiding.

But I'm not the only one to have noticed how brightly Kwame is shining. Joel strides over, half pretending that he's following the girl in Kwame's class with the plaited hair who now has the paper. But then he launches himself forward, grabbing hold of the exercise book that Kwame's clutching to his chest, and ripping it down the middle.

'No!' Kwame shouts, pages of his drawings scattering in the wind.

I stop running, bending breathlessly to help Kwame pick up some of the pages – mostly full of drawings of me and Kwame cycling, chasing, and waving from the window. Joel catches a few of the pages too, laughing loudly.

'Look, it's your diary!' he says. '*What do ghost foxes feel like?*' he reads. '*Does Nora have the same superpowers as a ghost hare?*'

'Give it back, please,' Kwame mutters, but Joel spins round, laughing.

'Ghost animals? So what – you can't make friends with living things, so you're hanging out with dead things – is that right, Barmy?'

For a moment, I wonder if Kwame is going to tell him that it's me who sees the ghosts – not him – but he doesn't. He just hangs his head. 'Please give it back; it's important.'

I clench my fists and march up behind Joel, snatching the pages out his hand before he even knows I'm there.

'That's right,' I say, so he wheels round. 'I have the same superpowers as an army of wild things with teeth. So you'd better leave my friend alone.'

Kwame frowns at me as Joel laughs nervously, looking around for support. But all the other children are still playing the Hare Race at the other end of the playground.

Kwame tries to pull me back. 'Nora, come on. Health and Fitness break is nearly over now anyway. Let's go back to the tree together.'

I shrug him off as Joel rounds on me, a snarl on his face.

'You know what they say about hares, don't you? That they're mad. You're mad as a March hare, Nora, just like Barmy.'

My blood seems to boil and fizz. 'Don't say that!' I shout. 'It's not nice calling people mad. Mental illness isn't a joke, you know.'

Kwame tries to pull me away again, pleading, 'Nora – come *on*. This isn't the way to do it. We're supposed to be the same.'

I don't know what he means about us being the same, but my fists are clenched now and Joel's eyes are glittering.

'You'd know all about being mad, wouldn't you?' he mutters. 'What with your crazy mum.'

It feels like Joel has punched me in the stomach. I step back, breath catching. I look around for Kwame, but he's already walking back to the tree on his own, his arms clutching his torn drawings, his head down. I think about running away with him too, when Joel laughs and swings his P.E. bag onto his back, walking away, and a new feeling leaps from my bones.

Anger.

I step forward as the ghost hare comes racing up behind me, rearing up on her hind legs and using her front paws to box, box, box. And I roar, chasing behind with my own fists raised. Together, we launch ourselves onto Joel's back, hitting and hitting his bag over and over again, so he yells out and tries to shake us off.

'Nora! Nora!'

Someone is calling my name, but my insides are a wild sea, and all I can see is rainbow and all I can feel is that cold nothing, deep inside my chest. And then hands are pulling me off Joel and I turn round to tell Kwame to get off and leave me alone – but it's not Kwame pulling me this time. It's the headteacher.

And I've never seen her so angry.

13

I've only ever been sent to the headteacher's office once before and that was back in Year One – a week after Dad left. I can't even remember why I was there now. There are rainbow edges to the memory though, and sharp, angry teeth.

I used to feel angry like that a lot, I think. When bad things happen, like your dad leaving for India, it's easier to be angry than it is sad. I find the rainbows confusing though, because I thought the ghost animals were here to make me feel strong – or at least less alone. But it felt like the ghost hare was showing me how to squeeze my fear into my fists and use them to hit, hit, *hit*.

Across the desk, Miss Rose the headteacher looks at Joel and me from over the top of her glasses. I'm expecting Joel to look bored, because he gets sent here all the time. But he looks small in the adult-sized chair and keeps his head down.

Miss Rose hasn't said anything yet, and I almost wish she would shout and scream and ask me what on earth I thought I was doing, because what she's doing now is way worse.

She looks concerned.

'Do you know why you're both here?'

I grip the foam padding on the chair. Joel keeps his head down and his mouth shut, so I say, 'Because we got into a fight.'

'That's right. And do you want to tell me why you were fighting?'

I think back to the ghost hare and the feelings that raged inside me. I look again to Joel and I see him look quickly at me, too. And I want to tell Miss Rose that Joel is a bully and said terrible, awful things about Mum – but I don't want to say them out loud again. So I just shrug.

Miss Rose pinches her lips. 'Are you both going to sit there and say nothing?'

Joel swings his legs in his chair. I shrug again.

She sighs. 'Look – I know you both have things going on at home right now, but that's not how we solve problems in this school, and it's not how we solve problems in the world either.'

My insides drop. From behind Miss Rose, I see a rainbow shape flit from the heater by the window and disappear behind the plant pot.

My heart races with it and I see Joel shoot his own panicked look at me. Under my flapping thoughts and worry that Miss Rose is going to talk about Mum's PTSD in front of a bully like Joel, a small voice also wonders what his home is like.

'I'm sorry,' I say quickly.

'I appreciate the apology, Nora, but I'd like to see you say that to Joel, please.'

I dart a look at Joel, but he doesn't look back at me. His eyes stay down at his swinging shoes. 'Sorry, Joel,' I say, quietly. Although I'm not sure I am. Not when he said what he said.

'And Joel?' Miss Rose says.

'Sorry,' he mumbles, but it doesn't sound like he

means it and I see the rainbow shape of the hare dart out again, paws out boxing, before running back under Miss Rose's desk.

My clenched fists bend my peeling plasters.

'I hope both of you know that if there's ever anything at home you want to talk about, everyone at this school is here for you? Miss Omar; your teacher Mr Richards, Joel; myself; every member of staff. We only want what's best for you.'

The hare darts again from under the desk, running to the door, only to find it closed, and doubles back on herself, ears flat and frightened.

'I'm *fine*,' I say, trying to steady my breathing. 'Can I go now?'

Miss Rose pinches her lips tight again. She stands up and I go to stand up too, thinking finally I'm free, but Joel stays sat on his seat.

'Nora, we take incidents like this very seriously at this school, as you know. We've called your parents, Joel, and your mum too, Nora. They're waiting outside.'

The room seems to spin for a moment.

'You called Mum?' I say as the hare whips round and round, bouncing off the walls.

'If you just wait here for a moment, I'm going to

step out and chat to them. And then, as it's nearly home time anyway now, I think it's best that you go back with them and use this time to think about your behaviour.'

I collapse back down on the chair as she leaves Joel and me alone. My heart is fluttering, my thoughts are racing, and still the ghost hare runs round the room, desperately trying to find a way out.

Mum is here. Which means Miss Omar will have had to call her and the phone will have rung, which might have made her jump. And now – Mum will think something is wrong, when it isn't.

The door closes and Joel sniffs.

'This is your fault,' I snap at him.

'You hit me!'

I roll my eyes. 'Only your bag. And you said . . .' I swallow. 'You bullied Kwame.'

Joel huffs and sinks down in his seat.

I go to say more, but outside we start to hear shouting voices. And I watch as Joel gets smaller and smaller in his chair as I stand up, racing to the exit with the ghost hare at my heels.

'Don't!' Joel shouts as I pull open the door.

But I have to, because there's shouting and it could

be Mum and her symptoms and I need to make it better again before anyone else sees.

But it's not Mum who's shouting. It's a tall man with round glasses and a short woman wearing hundreds of gold bangles that are smashing together like bits of broken glass. And they're not shouting at Miss Rose, but at each other, in huge voices all about Joel.

Joel's parents.

But that's not what makes the ghost hare flatten her ears and disappear back into the office, where Joel is trying to shut the door again. It's Mum – her head between her legs as she sits outside the office, clutching Kwame's hand next to her.

And he sees. And Miss Rose sees. And the receptionist and Joel's parents and Joel too.

I feel my face burning hot as I run over to Mum, pushing Kwame's hand away and putting mine in Mum's hand instead, kneeling down to whisper to her that it's okay and to breathe and also to be a bit quieter, because everyone is looking.

Miss Rose sits on Mum's other side, trying to make Mum feel better too, but she doesn't know what to do like I do. She doesn't understand that it's just Mum's symptoms and that her PTSD is making her think that things are worse than they are. And it doesn't mean that Mum isn't the strongest and best person in the world, and it doesn't mean that anything is wrong.

Everything is *fine*.

The receptionist tries to get me back into the office with Joel, but I shrug him off.

'She just needs you all to be quiet,' I say, louder than I should, so Mum raises her head to glare at me for being rude.

I'm almost relieved when she does that though, as it means Mum's panic attack isn't too bad. Sometimes, her PTSD can take her mind back in time and far away from me, but at least now she knows where she is.

Kwame's eyes are wide and I feel a jolt of anger as Mum starts to sit up, saying again and again that she's *fine* and that she's just being silly. I drop her hand and turn away as Miss Rose fusses over her, wondering if she should call an ambulance.

The rainbow hare panics again around my feet, jumping at the closed door like she too wants to run out of it far, far away. And I wish she would just *stop* and panic in a still way, like I'm having to do.

Kwame stands up, walking over to me.

'Nora?' he says, softly.

'You left me,' I snap at him. 'I stuck up for you and you left me alone.'

Kwame frowns. 'I didn't ask you to stick up for me. I thought you and me were the same and we could just run away and hide from all our problems together and—'

'I don't run away!' I shout, so Miss Rose stops talking and Mum winces again. Kwame tries to grab my hand, but I yank it away, my thoughts panicking in a circle with the hare. 'We're not the same. We're nothing alike at all.'

Kwame steps back like I've hit him, too.

I turn away and see the shouting couple and Joel and the receptionist and everyone looking at me. And I wish they would stop.

I grab Mum's hand. 'Come on, we need to go.'

Miss Rose is still talking about ambulances, but Mum's recovered enough now to tell her that we're okay. She's not doing a very good job of making them believe that though, and so I drag her quickly out of the school doors and across the playground, the hare racing ahead, until Mum pulls her hand out of mine.

'Nora! You're hurting me. What's going on with you?'

I spin round to her, my heart beating madly in my chest. 'Why did you have to come in and do that?'

Mum frowns. 'I got a call – your headteacher said you'd been in a fight. I—'

'But now they all think everything is wrong when it isn't! Why couldn't you just pretend you're normal, just whilst you were in there?'

Pigeons flap out of the trees next to us and Mum steps back, shocked. She's still in her around-the-house clothes and her eyes are puffy. And I keep thinking about her hand in Kwame's in the waiting room and the feeling is barbed and electric.

I kick a weed growing out of the kerb and stomp to the car, sitting in the seat and turning away from her as soon as she opens it.

She doesn't say anything all the drive home, so my thoughts race in circles. And when we get home, I run inside without her, so she has to chase me into the hall.

'Nora,' she sighs, closing the door. 'Nora, look at me, please.'

'I don't want to,' I mutter, kicking my shoes off.

I go to run up the stairs, but Mum catches me and tries to hug me. I push her away, but Mum holds me tighter, and she smells like home and it melts my anger like snow.

She squeezes me, tight. 'I'm so sorry, Nora. I'm sorry this is affecting you so much.'

I shake my head. 'It's not. I'm okay.'

Mum pulls away to look at me, putting my hair behind my ears. 'Fighting at school? Late slips? Nora – this isn't *okay*.'

'It wasn't my fault,' I say, quietly. 'The ghost hare—'

Mum sighs, pinching her eyes. 'Not these ghosts again, Nora. You're too old for this now. You need to take some responsibility for your actions.'

Behind her, the hare leaps.

She's right though. I need to be stronger for her if I'm ever going to help her get better.

I put my head down and nod, so Mum hugs me again, tightly.

'Oh, Nora. I'm sorry I embarrassed you in the office – I – it's this condition—'

'I know,' I say. 'It's not your fault, Mum.'

Mum rubs my back and sighs. 'I think we should make an appointment to see the doctor again together – is that okay with you?'

I want to tell her it isn't okay and that I'm *fine*. But

behind her, I see the ghost hare, finally stop running, about to lie down in the middle of the hall – her long body stretched out. And I realize how tired I am, too.

'Okay,' I say, in a small voice.

14

I don't get to sleep for ages. I keep thinking about Mum's hand in Kwame's and how I shouted, and it twists in my stomach like a snake. And so when I finally do get to sleep, I dream of pythons and ropes and tangled things.

I wake up to rain tapping on the window like long fingers and it takes me a moment to realize that the rainbow light in my room isn't coming from the sun sneaking through the drops, but from the ghost of a hare burrowing into my hair.

Insides leaping, my fingers twitch for my glasses,

but I still feel the snakes writhing between my ribs and hear Mum's words – that I'm too old for silly things like ghost hares now. I need to be responsible. I screw my eyes up tight, turning over and hiding away.

I feel the empty pressure of a tiny tongue licking my cheek, and it's the same cold not-cold feeling as when I first saw the ghost fox in my bed, but smaller. And it would be now that the ghost hare trusts me enough not to run away. Now she made me fight Joel and shout at Mum.

'Go away,' I snap.

The hare hops over my head to the other side of my pillow, one ear up and one down. I sit up, angrily.

'I don't want you here!' I whisper-shout. 'You and the ghost fox – you've ruined everything!'

The hare just looks at me, her head to the side.

Picking up my alarm clock, I throw it at her. She hops off the bed, but still doesn't go away.

'I don't understand why you're even here,' I say. 'It's not to make me strong. All you've done is panic and get angry and make everything worse.'

The hare hops closer to me, staring into that part of me I hide in the very back of my mind.

'All you've done is show me how bad things are.

And that maybe . . .' I take a deep breath as my insides tighten. 'And that maybe things aren't *fine* after all.'

The hare sits down, looking pleased with herself, and I turn away, closing my eyes, tight.

'Go away,' I whisper. 'I don't want to see you any more.'

The light seems to get a little dimmer suddenly. And when I open my eyes and look to the space on the floor where a ghost hare once sat, all I see now is emptiness.

PART THREE

THE RAVEN

15

I leave for school before Kwame can come to call for me. It's raining and even though it's not really a Good Morning, as Mum still looks haunted and tired, she says she wants to drive me so I'm there on time.

Not just there on time – I'm there before all the other cars have arrived.

'We're a bit early,' she says, checking her mirrors.

I undo my seat belt. 'That's okay,' I say. 'Miss Omar always gets into school early anyway and she lets me read on the beanbags when it's raining.'

Mum smiles and combs her hands through my hair. 'And you're okay, pal? We didn't get to chat much yesterday about the fight . . .'

I nod, my hand already on the door handle. 'It was just a mistake. Joel is a bully – I was just standing up to him.'

Mum smiles, but winces. 'That's good, Nora, but maybe next time—'

'—with words, not my fists, I know,' I say with a sigh, making Mum laugh and kiss my head.

'There's my girl,' she says.

I say goodbye and walk up the path. And there, sitting on the wall next to the entrance sign, is the ghost of a raven.

He has black-bead eyes, a sharp beak and dark, ruffled feathers. He's huge – much bigger than any bird I've ever seen this close – and I only know what he is from seeing pictures in books. Even though his feathers are dark, his ghost colours are racing red, blue and gold, and he's crouching like he's ready to pounce and take flight. Seeing him fills my whole insides with brightness for a moment, when I realize that Mum is still watching me.

I pretend quickly that I have a stone in my shoe and

then step very carefully round the raven to the door, keeping my head down. My heart is thumping, because up close I can see his intelligent eyes and huge claws and he's magnificent, but I also don't want to see ghost animals any more, so I throw open the door and run quickly inside.

I try to read my book on the beanbag in the classroom, but my thoughts are still whizzing. And when the rest of the class arrives, I try to keep my eyes on my work, but I can hear a ghostly tapping of feathers on the window.

At break, Miss Omar calls off outdoor play again, because of the rain. Around the growing puddles outside, I see two rainbow ravens now, ruffling their feathers and staring in at me.

I jump up from my desk and run over to the computers in the corner, before anyone else can get there to play games. In the search engine, I type:

FACTS ABOUT RAVENS

I learn that ravens are intelligent and great at hunting, and can even mimic human voices. But then I see that they are known to make lifelong enemies, and that a group of them is called an 'unkindness of ravens', so I quickly log off and give the computer to Rachael, who is waiting behind me, instead.

My stomach feels twisted because I'm not sure that the ravens aren't here to seek revenge on me for shouting at the hare last night and trying to ignore them. I keep my head down though until we stop lessons again for lunch and I sneak another peek outside. I almost shout out when I see the whole lawn outside our classroom covered in ghost birds – the most unkind unkindness of ravens I've ever seen – and they're all looking at me.

I run out of the classroom and down the corridor, trying to keep my eyes away from the windows. I'm almost expecting to be attacked by giant bird claws when I run right into Kwame in the canteen.

'Nora!' he says. 'Are you okay?'

I nod, dodging past him to get to the dinner queue.

'You don't seem okay. Are you still mad at me for running away yesterday? I am sorry, you know. I just got spooked because you didn't want to do the same thing as me. And . . .' He looks down at his feet. 'Also, you sticking up for me made me feel a bit pathetic.'

He mumbles the last thing, but I'm not really listening. I'm trying to focus on what other types of vegetables I want with my pie and ignore the dark feathers gathering at the windows. The silence stretches like a big elastic band, and Kwame reaches out for my hand, but I pull it away.

'I told you, I don't need your help,' I snap at him.

He frowns, confused. 'But I'm not saying—'

'Just go away!' I say, a bit louder than I wanted to. 'Go play your silly games – I want to be on my own.'

Kwame looks hurt, so I growl and get a sandwich from the counter instead, running to go and eat it in the toilets where boys and ravens aren't allowed.

My thoughts are muddled round each other. I still feel embarrassed that Kwame saw Mum like that, and that he held her hand when that's my job. It's all tangled with other thoughts too, like the unkindness of ravens waiting for me, and how the ghost hare made me realize that things aren't *fine*, and it's all a lot to carry around in just one chest.

I know one thing though – the ghost animals have brought nothing but trouble. After the fox appeared in my room, all my careful lines have been blurred and everything has got worse. I lost my bike and Mum got angry with me. I got into a fight and everyone saw that she's struggling.

I just want everything to go back to normal.

I think about staying in the toilets all day, but then I hear the beat of feathers on the window. I can feel hundreds of black-bead eyes on me as I run back to my classroom, so I keep my head so far down that I run straight into Miss Omar at the door of the classroom.

'Nora, you might have more luck walking around with your head up.'

'Sorry, Miss Omar,' I say, rubbing my arm.

She bends down to find my eyes under my fringe and she frowns. 'Are you okay?'

She says it quietly, like a secret.

I nod quickly and try to run past her, but I can tell she's watching me all the way back to my seat. And I can tell she's watching me all through lessons too.

At the end of the school day, I try to zip out without her noticing, but of course she spots me.

'Nora? Can I have a word, please?'

I shuffle over to her desk slowly whilst everyone else packs away and lines up to leave. And when they're gone, the silence between us feels as empty as deep space.

Miss Omar smiles at me and sits on the edge of her desk, her arms folded. She's wearing a short headscarf today that seems to shimmer with different rainbow colours as it catches the light from the window.

'You know you can talk to me, Nora.'

She doesn't say it like a question, so I don't say anything back. She waits for me though, so eventually I sigh.

'I don't have anything to talk about.'

Miss Omar looks like she doesn't believe me. But she leans back across her desk and gets a raven-covered notebook out of her desk drawer.

My heart leaps.

'You know,' she says, 'sometimes, I feel like I have so many thoughts that I'm not sure which one to think first. And although the best thing to do when I feel like that is tell someone I trust, sometimes I find it can be helpful first to write them down.'

She flicks through the notebook, and inside are pages and pages of neat handwriting in all different colours of pen.

'You wrote all of that?'

She nods, smiling. 'Over a whole school term though. But it's not about how much I write; it's about giving myself a blank space to tell myself the truth.'

Suddenly, she rips a big chunk of pages out of the book and I shout a bit without meaning to.

'Miss Omar!' I say, my mouth open.

She laughs and hands the half-empty notebook to me, her own words now coverless and torn on her desk. 'Don't tell anyone I did that.'

I stare at the book and then stare at her until she gently shoves it into my chest.

'Take it. Write words. And then when you're ready, show someone you trust what you've written. And I hope you know you can trust me, Nora. Teachers are here to teach, but we're also here to listen.'

I take the book from her and she goes back round her desk to tidy up.

I'm not sure what to do. A teacher just ripped a book and here I am with the evidence. But also, the ravens on the cover look different on the book – less like enemies. More like friends.

I look outside to see the ravens all taking flight, turning the sky into a flutter of dark rainbow.

'Thank you,' I say quietly, putting the notebook in my bag.

16

When I get home, Mum is using her too-polite telephone voice in the hall and seems relieved to see me come in and drop my school bag.

'Ah, here she is now,' she says, giving me a secret eye-roll as the person keeps talking to her. 'Yes,' she says, before using her fake laugh. 'Okay, well, bye then. Okay. Yes. Bye!'

She quickly holds the phone out to me, whispering, 'It's your dad.'

I kick off my shoes, my eyes wide. Usually Mum

never speaks to Dad on the phone if she can help it. I always thought that was because it made her sad, but it looks like she actually finds him boring.

'He's calling on a terrible line – typical.'

I snatch the phone from her.

'Dad?' I say, running upstairs and shutting my bedroom door, breathlessly.

'Nora!' Dad sings, his voice faraway and jittery. 'How's my wildcat daughter?'

'You sound different,' I say, trying to turn the volume up.

'It's not the best line . . .'

But it's not just that. His accent sounds different too. He's always sung my name, but now his other words sound unusual, like he's from a whole other place. Maybe he is now.

'I miss you,' I say. I bite my lip, because although I speak to Dad sometimes on the phone, I've not seen him since he left years ago, so it feels like a strange thing to say.

'Oh,' he says, clearing his throat. 'Well, yes – me too. Although work is keeping me busy! We have some new tiger cubs on the reserve whose mother abandoned them, so they're keeping us up day and night.'

I sit down on the bed as the line crackles.

Dad clears his throat again. 'Actually, just on that – your mum just asked if I was planning to come back for a bit. And – well – I can if you need me to, Nora . . . but the cubs are really young still and the team here are stretched. But hey – if you're struggling—'

'We don't need help,' I say, quickly. 'You don't need to come back, Dad – it sounds like you're really busy.'

A shadow passes over the window and I turn away to the wall.

Dad laughs. 'Yeah . . . Um – but you're sure you're okay? Because your mum was just telling me about some sort of fight at school . . .'

'Oh,' I say, blocking my ear from feathers tapping at the window. 'You know me, Dad. I'm a wildcat – I can look after myself.'

Dad laughs again, talking about the other animals he's looking after and the death-defying adventures he's been on to save bison from sinkholes and sloth bears from hunters. The line is bad though and I only catch a few words, so after a while I stop listening, and only tune back in when he says the word 'grandma'.

'Grandma . . . if you want to . . . lots of animals . . . excuse the mess.'

'What?' I say, squinting. 'I can't hear you.'

'The line is . . . just saying . . . get in touch again . . .'

The line crackles and goes dead, just as I hear a loud thump on the window, making me jump and turn round. Outside, the ravens I saw at school are all cawing, their ghostly noise only just getting through the glass, but the thud of their claws and bodies is making my lightshade rattle.

I run downstairs to see if Mum can hear too, when a loud, urgent knock hammers on our front door. I rush to answer, expecting to see feathers, but instead, panting on the doorstep, there's a sweaty-looking Kwame, his fist still in the air.

'Go a—' I start to say.

'It's my grandad! My grandad – he's – please – I don't know what—'

My heart leaps to my mouth and I open the door all the way so Kwame can come in, but he pulls me out, even though I don't have any shoes on.

'What's wrong?' Mum says behind me, staring out at Kwame looking wild and lost and afraid.

'It's my grandad,' he says again. 'He's had a fall.'

I grip Kwame's hand and squeeze it tight. I look back at Mum, but she's disappeared into the house and for a moment, I'm afraid. But then she comes back with the same bright green first-aid kit she used to plaster up my wounds when I fell off the bike.

'Mum—' I start to say.

'Shoes, Nora,' she says, handing them to me – hers somehow already on. She smiles at Kwame like she's known him for ages, and puts her hand on his shoulder. 'Can you take me to him?'

Kwame nods, still looking scared, but he leads Mum across the road as I hurriedly pull on my shoes and close the door, scrambling after them.

We walk through the hallway again and into the mishmash kitchen, a strange burst of colour in a moment that feels black and white.

Kwame clatters to the back door and takes us into the wild garden towards the broken caravan at the back, and I feel a twist of sickness when we see Kwame's grandad lying on the cracked path around the side of the caravan, looking like he's in pain.

'It's okay, Grandad, I've brought help like I said,' Kwame says in a quiet voice.

His grandad looks confused at Kwame, Mum and me. 'Who are you?' he says. 'I'm *fine*, honestly – I don't need any h—' But he sucks in his breath in pain as he tries to move.

Mum steadies him and I look around, not sure what to do. On the grass next to us, a single ghost raven tips his head to the side, nudging his beak towards a piece of paper and a pen.

I reach over to grab it, writing in big letters.

Nora Frost —
Kwame's friend

I stick it down my top again and Kwame's grandad reads it, looking a little less confused. Kwame reads it too, looking at me.

I'm sorry, I mouth at him.

Kwame bends and squeezes my hand tight.

Mum opens her first-aid kit, speaking loudly and clearly to Kwame's grandad and then checking his eyes and head gently. It's like she has a rainbow glow around her – like she's come back to life and here she is, helping people again, and everything is back the way it should be.

Miri Frost –
Paramedic

I stick the paper on Mum's chest and she gives me a little sideways smile before looking at Kwame.

'You've done so well, Kwame, for coming to get help. Your grandad looks okay, but I think we might want to take him to hospital just to make sure. Do you know how to call an ambulance?'

Kwame nods. 'Dial 999? I've not done it before.'

'Nora will show you – won't you, Nora?'

I nod, taking Mum's mobile phone and squeezing Kwame's cold hand tight.

'It's okay,' I say. 'Mum's a paramedic – she knows what she's doing. It sounds like your grandad is going to be fine.' I smile at him and he nods. He still looks a little shaky, so I sit him down off the path, away from Mum now making jokes with Kwame's grandad, and dial 999 on her phone.

'Do you want me to speak to them?' I ask him.

He shakes his head. 'I can do it.'

I hand the phone to him as it begins to ring. 'You absolutely can.'

Kwame keeps hold of my hand as he speaks to the man on the other end. The man asks questions about the address, and I help Kwame with the postcode, because it's the same as mine. He also asks what happened to his grandad, and Kwame says that when he came home from school, he found his grandad on the ground in the garden, so I squeeze his hand extra tight. Then the man asks to speak to Mum, who tells him all about how his vitals look good, but how there is some pain in his hip.

Kwame does a great job telling Mum everything about all the medication his grandad is on and has drawings of all the bottles in his notebook, even though some of the bottles have scaly tails and are breathing fire.

'You're a good one to have around!' Mum says, and his grandad reaches out and grabs Kwame's hand tightly.

'The best.'

Kwame beams.

The ambulance will take a while to come. Kwame tries to call his house phone to let his parents know, but no one picks up. He doesn't want to leave his grandad's side, so we go inside to fetch blankets and make tea whilst we wait for the ambulance. We all sit in the garden together on the path, and even though it's not a party, as Kwame's grandad is still on the floor and still in a bit of pain, it feels much nicer than it should. And that's all thanks to Mum, who makes everyone laugh and feel safe.

When the ambulance arrives, Mum goes off to meet them at the front door, and Kwame's grandad closes his eyes for a moment in the setting sun.

'Your mum is amazing,' Kwame says.

I smile. 'She is, isn't she?'

'I didn't realize she was a paramedic. You must feel really proud of her.'

I blush, but nod too, because I really do. And

Kwame's hand is still tight in mine, just like it was in Mum's when she needed him, and so I tell him the truth too. 'Do you know what PTSD is?'

Kwame shakes his head and I lick my lips because they're feeling dry.

'It means—'

'Post-traumatic stress disorder,' Kwame's grandad says out of nowhere, his eyes still closed.

Kwame smiles and nudges his grandad. 'Show-off,' he says, and his grandad opens his eyes briefly to wink at him.

'How do you know that?' I ask him.

He smiles. 'It's like I said to you before, Nora – you can learn a lot from the written word.'

'What is it?' Kwame asks me.

I think back to what Mum and the doctor told me before Christmas. 'Sometimes, when someone sees something bad or stressful, the memory of it can stay with them. Last year, my mum was racing around being a paramedic and she had to see a lot of sad and stressful situations. Sometimes the ghosts of that come back to her and it can make her feel really sad too, or angry, or afraid. Like you saw the other day.'

Kwame nods, his eyes wide. 'So she sees ghosts, too?'

I look over to the door, where voices are following Mum, walking back through the hall. 'They're a different kind of ghost. A kind of memory. But she's getting help and she's taking some time off being a paramedic whilst she gets better.'

Kwame sighs heavily. 'She's even more amazing than I thought!'

I smile wide and I sit up straight. Kwame's grandad puts his hand out too and clamps it over both of ours, his eyes now fully open.

'I may not remember everything,' he says, 'but I know for a fact that PTSD is nothing to be ashamed of, Nora.'

I feel a lot of things all at once and they get rammed up in my throat, so I can't say thank you or any of the things I probably should say. But then Mum is here with the paramedics in their bright green outfits and we step away so they can help.

Kwame and I watch them roll his grandad onto a stretcher. And it feels brilliant to see Mum helping like it's the most natural thing she can ever do and I feel so proud I could burst.

'Well, I do feel like a weak old fool,' Kwame's grandad says, as they take him up the path.

Mum smiles warmly. 'Now, Erwin – there's nothing weak about getting a bit of a helping hand when you need it.' She catches my eye and her smile fades slightly, her eyes darting back down at her feet.

Behind me, the ghost raven caws and this time, I turn to look properly at it – its feathers shining in its own rainbow light.

17

Before the ambulance leaves with Kwame's grandad safely inside, Kwame and I run to his house to tell his parents what's happening.

It's down the hill and round the bend, but it looks just the same as all the other houses on my street from the outside. Inside though, there are boys charging round the hall, climbing stairs and shouting.

'This is your house?' I giggle.

Kwame rolls his eyes and it feels funny that someone who loves being alone as much as Kwame could live in a house that's so busy.

'That's why I'm always at Grandad's,' he says.

He leaves me in a hall filled with coats and toys – baby John crawling over to cling onto my leg at the door. Inside the living room, Owen and Payne are now shouting and wrestling on the floor, and someone else I can't see is trying to hush them from the kitchen, cooking something that smells sweet and makes my tummy rumble.

I hear Kwame speak with them and all the busyness suddenly stops.

'Everyone out!' a man's voice booms.

The boys in the living room stop wrestling and even baby John stops trying to crawl up my leg, and everyone is suddenly in the hall with me, putting on coats and shoes, and Kwame is right – everything does smell a bit like feet.

The man who was in the kitchen is wearing a rainbow-coloured tie round his long locs, but he looks worried as he opens the door.

'Kwame – can you lock up please, son?'

Kwame nods and the man goes running out, his long coat billowing behind him as he races up the hill.

Without him there, things get busy again, with baby

John screaming and Owen and Payne back to fighting again.

'Hey, that's my coat!' Payne shouts.

'You're standing on my toes!' Owen says.

'No, no, no!' baby John shouts over them.

It's all quite a lot, but Kwame is very calm. He sorts out the right coats, picks up his baby brother and locks the door behind us all.

'Nora, you remember all my brothers. Well, nearly all of them – Izaak will be doing his paper round.'

'Yes, hi,' I say, shyly.

Owen gives me a small wave and Payne slaps me on the back as we all follow Kwame up the hill to his grandad's house, only going silent when they see their dad climbing into the ambulance with their grandad.

'Kwame – can you look after your brothers, please? I've let your mum know – she's on her way back from work now.'

Kwame nods, but Mum puts her hand over his shoulder. 'It's okay, they can come to ours for a bit. We'll keep an eye on them.'

Kwame's dad nods at her and the ambulance is closed and driven away.

Mum looks round at all the children she suddenly

has, and for a moment I'm worried that they're going to be too busy for her ghosts to handle. But Mum is still in super-mode, and she takes baby John off Kwame like she's his real mum and shouts, 'Who wants chicken nuggets?' over the bickering of the other two.

Everyone charges into our house and all the curtains are opened. Mum takes baby John into the kitchen to cook, and I stick the TV onto cartoons for Owen and Payne, but they're not really interested. Instead, Kwame takes down a dusty board game we haven't played since Saffie used to come over, and we all play that.

It's loud, but it's brilliant. Owen is a lot younger than us, but he's really clever. Payne struggles to sit still, but he laughs loudly any time I say a joke like it's really funny. It's nice to see Kwame smiling again after what happened with his grandad, and even nicer to see them all digging into chicken nuggets and chips when Mum brings them through.

Mum sits on the floor with us and laughs loudly with Payne, disappearing only to answer the door and invite a lady in who's wearing a bright pink suit and must be Kwame's mum. She kisses everyone's heads and picks up baby John.

'You must be Nora,' she says, clutching my hand. She

has the same soft golden-brown skin Kwame has and I smile shyly at her. 'We've heard so much about you.'

I look at Kwame, who looks a bit embarrassed, but he shakes his head, because he knows I'm thinking about the ghost animals. I'm pleased that's not the thing they all know about me.

My mum and Kwame's mum sit on the sofa together and the living room is a firework of noise and laughter and bright colours. And when Kwame's mum stands up and says it's time to go, I join in with all the groaning.

Payne tips over the game board and Kwame helps me tidy everything away, his tiger-striped socks matching mine exactly.

'Why do you wear those?' I ask him as we put the counters back in the box.

Kwame looks away. 'I saw you wearing them when we first met and I thought tiger stripes could be like our uniform. It's been really nice knowing someone who's like me.'

I think back to how I pushed him away after the fight. 'I'm sorry for being so grumpy before, Kwame. But you know – we don't have to be exactly the same for us to be friends. I like that you're a slightly different kind of weird.'

He grins wide.

Whilst Kwame's mum takes over getting everyone's shoes on again, he hangs back to speak to my mum.

'Thank you for your help today,' he says. 'Will my grandad be okay?'

Mum squeezes his shoulder, bending down. 'Thanks to you, I think he'll be fine. The doctors will take care of him now.'

Kwame nods, following his family outside to a song of *thank-you*s and *see-you-soon*s. Mum and I stand on the doorstep waving them off, and I give a special wave just to Kwame.

'What a lovely lot,' Mum says. 'How do you know Kwame?'

I watch them go round the corner. 'He's my friend.'

18

For the rest of the week at school,
Kwame and I meet under our weeping
cherry tree every break and lunch,
sitting with our backs together
and eating the brightly coloured
salads his mum always makes
too much of.

Some leaves are starting
to grow on the tree now
and I find it easier and

easier to talk and laugh with Kwame. He updates me on his grandad's progress at the hospital and I help him understand all the medical terms like 'intravenous fluids' and 'MRI'. Thankfully though, it turns out his grandad didn't break anything when he fell over, and by Friday, he's back home with a new button that he wears around his neck and can press if he needs any help. It sends a signal to Kwame's parents' phones, so then they can rush over straight away.

'What does your grandad think about that?' I ask him, as we finish our Friday lunch.

I feel him shrug behind me. 'I told you – he's rubbish at asking for help. But we're hoping that the button reminds him that we're here if he does need anything. And not just from me, but from Mum, Dad and the whole rest of the family too – together.'

There's a breeze outside the tree and it rustles the new leaves on it, making it sound like we're in the middle of an amphitheatre. Kwame says blossom buds will grow on the branches with the leaves soon, and I can't wait to sit here with him underneath a fountain of flowers.

Meanwhile, I tell Kwame about the unkindness of ghost ravens.

'I thought they were there to punish me for shouting and ignoring them, but now I'm not sure. I think maybe they were trying to warn me that your grandad needed help.'

Kwame looks thoughtfully at me. 'You always speak about them like they're real-life creatures.'

I frown at him. 'They are . . . I told you that before and you said you believe me . . . Don't you?'

Kwame looks like he's thinking about that carefully and I start to get cross again when he finally nods. 'It makes sense that they were trying to warn you – ravens are very clever. My grandad actually invented a game about them called Guess the Raven. You have to ask someone ten yes-or-no questions to find out what animal they're thinking of.' He digs around his pockets for pencils. 'If I ever saw a ghost raven, I'd probably think it was trying to show me something, or lead me to some answers.' He stops to look at me in that way he does again, like he's reading all my thoughts. 'Is there an answer you're looking for, Nora?'

I frown, searching my bag for my apple. 'Maybe . . .'

Kwame pinches his lips and starts drawing feathers. My hand closes round the raven journal that Miss Omar gave me. I've not written in it yet, but as Kwame is busy drawing pictures of the ghost raven now, I start writing on the first page and try my best to tell the truth.

I write about how I saw the fox and all the animals I've seen since – and how it might be nice to finally start getting some answers about why they're here. I write about losing my bike and how it slipped between my fingers. I write about Kwame and his special kind of weird, and then I start writing about Mum.

It's difficult to tell the truth about Mum because I love her and think she's the best person in the world. But also, there's a knot inside my heart when I think about her PTSD and how she's not always out of bed when I come home from school. Writing about that feels like I'm betraying her somehow.

When the bell goes for the end of lunch, I read back the last few lines I wrote and my heart sinks.

There on the page are the worst words I've ever thought. And the very last line makes me want to tear the page out and screw it up and make sure no one ever reads it.

'Are you coming, Nora?' Kwame asks, holding the branches of the tree back for me.

I snap the book closed quickly, my heart beating in my ears, and stuff it at the very bottom of my bag.

I think about that terrible last line a lot during afternoon lessons and I'm still deep in thought about it when Kwame rides us home on his bike.

'What's wrong?' he says, like he can read my mind again.

'Nothing,' I say, quickly.

I'm not sure he believes me, as he takes a detour off the cycle path home and onto the canal, where there are bright white swans swimming over the place my bike lies at the bottom. It's nice though, and it's fun riding up and down the bridges with him. And when we go under the tunnels, we shout both our names together and they swoop and combine in the echo into one.

I lift my head to the sky as we race out of one of the tunnels. For a moment, the brightness on the other side blinds me, and so I try to blink the shape out of my eye for a long time before I realize what it is.

'The ghost raven is back again!' I shout in Kwame's ear.

Kwame stops so fast, we're almost both thrown into the canal, and he looks around wildly like he might be able to spot it.

'Where? Where?'

I point up into the sky where the raven is circling over our heads – his rainbow edges glittering in the sunlight. He's huge – his wings flapping and his body like a shadow, with a hooked beak. I look around for any others, but it's just him here alone this time, his dark eyes fixed on me.

'He's beautiful,' I whisper.

Kwame looks at me. 'Do you think he's here to give you some answers?'

The raven dives when he hears this, so I duck out of the way before his ghost wings brush my face. He caws out – and it's that same strange echo noise I heard round the fox when she barked at me – like he's in a long tunnel.

And then he flies away.

'He's going back that way!' I shout at Kwame, pointing back where we just came.

Kwame tries to turn the bike round, but I jump off, looking towards home.

'I can't follow,' I say, twisting the edges of my school jumper. 'Mum might get worried about where I am . . .'

I think about her face when I came home from the canal last time, battered and bruised. Kwame bites his lip before he jumps off his bike, handing me the handlebars.

'I'll run and tell your mum where you are. You go follow the bird on my bike.'

I look at him wide-eyed. 'But—'

'It's fine,' he says, already running away. 'I'll catch up with you! My bike has a tracker on it.'

Kwame is strangely fast suddenly and he rockets away from me. I dither on the spot for a moment, torn between following him and also following the bird. But there's something deep inside me that feels like the raven has caught a thread in my insides that he's pulling away, away, and I want to get it back. I want to get some answers. About why the ghost animals are here. About what they're trying to show me.

About how I can help Mum get better.

I jump on Kwame's bike, which isn't like riding mine was at all, as it only has half the number of gears and no suspension. But it goes surprisingly fast and I take off after the bird, my insides soaring with it like I've found my wings again.

I whoop under the tunnels and pump my legs so fast, I've soon caught up with the raven and we're flying together. He swerves around me, playing in the wind

I'm cutting on the bike, cawing over and over like he's talking to me.

We get to the bit where I lost my bike before and, this time, I slow down enough to not get distracted when the raven flies up the bank and into the trees.

I can't ride the bike up there, so I get off and push it through the long grass, thorns scratching at my legs and tangling in the wheel spokes. But then I get to the path and scramble back on the bike, following the raven down towards the railway line that snakes through the valley.

It's been ages since I've been on a train. The last time might even have been before Dad left, so the memory of it feels strange and far away in my mind. I think about it though as I ride down to the bottom, where a wooden gate separates the path from the railway line. A sign on it points down a set of wooden stairs, across the thick metal railway tracks and up again on the other side. And although the sign says it's a footpath, the gate is plastered with other signs, too.

STOP - LOOK - LISTEN

BEWARE OF TRAINS

WARNING:
DANGER OF DEATH

DO NOT TRESPASS ON THE RAILWAY

The raven flaps onto the gate, cawing at me loudly. I'm panting hard as I stop the bike, my hair sweaty under my helmet. I stay sat on it though, watching the raven as he hops left and right as if talking to me in a kind of bird dance.

'I'm not following you down there – it's dangerous.'

He caws angrily at me, and I caw angrily back at him.

'No! It's not even just a bit dangerous, but the kind of dangerous that puts everything in my whole world at risk, and I won't do it.'

The raven turns his back to me and I huff and puff back at him, throwing Kwame's bike down and storming off to go sit under a tree with my arms crossed.

My thoughts are angry at the raven and also at everything else, because I want to follow him to find the answers to all my questions, but I promised Mum that I would keep myself safe. And I'm mad at Kwame for not being here and also mad at Mum for being the reason why.

I think about my notebook in the bottom of my bag and take it out. I don't look at the terrible words I wrote at lunchtime, but open a new page and start writing outside the lines in a very messy way.

IT'S NOT FAIR,
IT'S NOT FAIR,
it's not
fair.

It feels like kicking and thrashing, and after five goes at writing it, I start to feel a bit calmer – like I'm pulling a thorn out of my hand.

I write it a few more times anyway, and when I look up, the raven is perched on my school bag, staring at me with his head cocked to one side.

He looks even bigger close up. He has a long, straight beak with feathers stretching across half the top. He doesn't keep still either, but hops and twitches, all the time watching me.

I'm not afraid of him though. Kwame doesn't think he's here to hurt me, and I think he might be right.

I put my hand out. The raven eyes me cautiously, but then ducks down, presenting his back to my fingers. I suck in my breath and reach down to feel that same something-nothing cold numbness I felt with the other animals.

I stroke him twice and then he puts his head back up, cocking it again to the side like he's saying, *Are you happy now?*

I smile, looking up the path to see if Kwame is here yet, but he isn't. I think about his grandad's Guess the Raven game. Now I'm here alone with the raven though, a lot of my questions feel too big suddenly to ask out loud.

'Do you know the fox and the hare?' I ask instead.

He caws at me, but I don't speak raven, so I pull a browning apple core from my lunch box and hold it out to him instead. 'The fox didn't eat the lasagne I made. Can you eat anything?'

He snaps his beak at the apple and it's strange, because he never quite reaches it – like he's always that bit too far away.

'I suppose you can't, then.'

The raven hops back on my bag and I notice the white ring round his foot with numbers on the side.

'Did you belong to someone?' I ask.

He caws at me in a way that says he is a wild thing and couldn't ever belong to anyone. But also, the way he is around me makes me think he might be used to people – a lot more than the hare at least. She was frightened of everything.

I clear my throat. 'Why can I see you? Why now?'

He looks at me for a moment. And then he flaps his big wings into the air, ducking and diving over the fence towards the railway.

I jump up, my arm out like I might be able to grab him back and make him stay. But he's just a raven, and however much I want him to answer my questions, he can't talk to me.

I do hear a voice though, coming from the direction the raven flew in, so I walk slowly back

towards the gate and look down
the steep steps, over the metal railway
tracks to the other side, where Joel is using a
huge stick that's almost as tall as he is to whack a
tree, over and over again.

'It's not fair! It's not fair!' he shouts, using his whole
body to swing the stick back and whack it onto the thick
tree trunk, so the new leaves on the branches shudder
and shake.

A wave of anger rises up inside me, because it's
Joel and he's a bully and I don't like him. But
then there's a strange, confused feeling that
whirlpools round it, because those are the
same words I just wrote down in my raven
journal.

Joel gives a final roar and throws the

stick towards the railway, where it bounces off the steps and right onto the railway line.

Joel looks at it, his breath heaving. The stick is right across both of the tracks, one end hooked on the metal. I think about shouting at him for being stupid, when we hear a huge horn blare, making us both jump high into the air.

The train. The train is hurtling towards the stick on the tracks. I see all the colour drain from Joel's face as he looks between the stick and the train around the bend, travelling so fast that the forest on either side shakes and dances in its wake.

'No!' I shout, leaping towards the gate.

But Joel can't hear me over the stampede of carriages. He slips down the bank towards the stairs, taking them two at a time towards the final gate at the end separating him from the stick on the tracks.

He pushes the gate and I shout louder than I ever have in my whole life.

'LEAVE IT! Trains don't stop for anything!'

I see a flash of pale surprise as the train thunders between us, smashing the stick to smithereens.

19

I feel sick as I wrench myself away from the gate, doubling over and thinking, *No, no no no*.

All my bones are full and fizzing with adrenaline. My insides feel weak and watery. And my legs feel impossibly numb.

Joel. Joel was going to the train line. He was going to pick up the stick I watched turn to sawdust under the train's unstoppable wheels.

And I don't know that he didn't. All I saw was the flash of a pale face before the train whipped it away.

Sinking to the ground, I think of Mum, of how she might feel when her PTSD comes. And I wonder if it feels like this – panic.

'I could have got it, you know,' Joel says from behind me.

I scramble up, my words still lost. He's alive – on my side of the valley now – holding onto the fence like he might fall down otherwise.

'You – you—' I take a deep breath and swallow. 'You could have died!'

Joel frowns. 'I was only trying to help, you know. I thought the stick would have toppled the train over.'

He looks over the edge of the fence and I step shakily to look with him. The stick lies in splinters across the tracks.

I push him, angry again. 'Why would you put yourself at risk like that?'

Joel steps back, his fists clenching. 'Hey!'

But the adrenaline is leaving me tired and angry, so I push him away from the gate towards my backpack under the tree. 'You could have got hurt, Joel. And your parents . . .'

Joel's face clouds over and I remember the shouting people from that time in the headteacher's office, and what he said when he was beating the tree.

I put my head down. 'I – I'm sorry—'

'You don't know anything about my parents!' he shouts.

He bends and picks up my school bag from the ground, tipping everything out so my things go tumbling.

'Hey!' I shout, marching to snatch it off him, but he fishes out the raven notebook and I freeze.

He notices, a smile now back on his face.

He opens it to the page I wrote under the tree at lunch. The one with those terrible words. I want to shout, but my words have disappeared again.

'*I wish Mum would be my mum again*,' Joel reads, in a mock-whiney voice. '*I wish I didn't have to be so grown up all the time.*'

My blood boils hot and I should be ripping and raging at him like a wild thing, all teeth and claws for reading that out. For saying those words. But I wrote them, and hearing them out in the world makes me feel empty inside.

Joel laughs. He lifts the book higher, getting ready to shout the whole thing out and I know what comes next. I remember writing it.

That final, terrible line.

Suddenly I hear a roar from behind me and a speeding

figure jumps over me, tackling Joel to the floor, so the notebook goes skidding out of his hands. I scramble to pick it up, clutching it to my chest as the two figures scuffle on the ground.

Kwame.

'That's my friend! That's my friend!' Kwame shouts over and over.

Joel tries to get up, but Kwame keeps him pinned, shuffling around on the floor like his brothers were doing in the living room.

Eventually, my bones unstick and I grab Kwame by the arm and pull him up, even though he was probably winning and I'm quite impressed.

Joel scrambles to his feet, his ears bright red. 'You'll pay for that, Barmy!'

'It's Kwame!' Kwame shouts, dirt all over his face. 'You know my name and you know you're a bully, Joel.'

'She's the bully!' he shouts, pointing at me. 'She's the one who hit me in the playground and started on at me about my parents getting divorced! She's the one who . . . who . . .'

And then Joel does something that makes Kwame and I suck in our breath and hold it.

He bursts into tears.

Kwame and I look at each other.

'I didn't say anything about his parents,' I mumble to Kwame, wide-eyed. 'I just said they might be worried if he got hurt . . .'

'Yeah, well, they wouldn't!' Joel says, his face scrunched. 'They don't notice anything I do because they're always shouting at each other, all the time. And now they're getting a divorce and it's all my fault.'

He says the last bit like he's finally crossed the finish line of a very long race, and he crumbles to the ground, his head in his hands.

I put my own head down and pick at my plasters, but Kwame steps forward, sitting down next to Joel and carefully putting his arm around him. And I expect Joel to push him off and say something nasty, but he actually leans into Kwame, his shoulders shaking.

I suddenly feel awful. For hitting Joel's bag in the playground. For not seeing that he's just angry and scared and lonely and thinks that nothing is fair. Just like me.

I step forward and sit down, so we're all in a circle.

'My parents are divorced, too,' I say, quietly.

Joel puts his head up, wiping his eyes. 'They are?'

I nod. 'I was only five when it happened, but I

remember feeling . . . cross. And lonely.'

I look for ghost wings, but see nothing but blue sky and fluffy white clouds, moving overhead like nothing is happening below them.

Joel nods, sadly. 'I just want everything to go back to normal,' he says.

My journal is still tucked under my arm and I can feel the words I wrote like burning-hot coals. *It's not fair.*

'It can't though,' I whisper.

I finally hear the flutter of ghost wings and look to see the raven perched on the branches above us.

I swallow.

'It's happening and it's not okay. But you don't have to deal with it by yourself.'

Kwame is looking at me and I wish he wouldn't.

The raven caws, fluttering down to land in the middle of the circle, looking at me. And I wish Joel and Kwame could see the inky black of his feathers and the way his colours soar.

'It's true – you're not alone,' Kwame says, nudging Joel. 'We're here. As your friends.'

Joel sniffs, nodding.

The raven looks at me. And I close my eyes tight and nod too, because I think I know the answer now. To why the ghost animals are here. And why now.

I just don't know if I'm brave enough to tell myself yet.

Kwame pushes his shoe into mine as a sort of foot hug. And when I open my eyes, I catch the glint of rainbow-black wings, disappearing into the clouds.

20

Joel walks back up the path with us in silence, but when we come to the top of the cycle path near where he lives, he sticks his hands in his pockets and kicks at the dirt under his trainers.

'Thanks for saving my life,' he mumbles.

My insides flip when I remember the train, but I shrug. 'Thanks for telling us about your parents.'

He nods, but keeps his head low as he turns and leaves us, hands still in his pockets as he walks down the road.

'You saved his life?!' Kwame says, passing me my helmet. 'What happened when I was gone?'

'Oh, nothing,' I say, freezing when I remember why he wasn't there for it. 'Mum! Did you speak to her? Was she okay?'

He holds his breath and looks at me before speaking. 'There was a note on the door . . .'

He hands it to me, but I don't open it because I know what it'll say.

We cycle in silence for a while, our stomachs rumbling for dinner. We pass a pair of magpies squabbling in the trees and I remember how Kwame stuck up for me when Joel was reading from my notebook, and how he stopped Joel reading that final, terrible line.

'Why don't you stick up for yourself like you stood up for me earlier?' I say in his ear. 'You're quite good at wrestling.'

He laughs. 'I'm only good because of my brothers; I don't really like it. I just got so cross seeing him do that. I guess it made me brave somehow.'

I smile. 'Maybe you should get brave like that for yourself every once in a while, too.'

I can sense he's thinking about that as we cycle the final bit towards home.

'Did you catch up with the raven?' he asks. 'Did you find your answers?'

I roll my eyes. 'I caught up with him, but he wanted me to follow him over the railway line and it was too dangerous.'

'Oh,' Kwame says, disappointedly. 'Why would he take you down there?'

I shrug. 'The ghost animals have all led me to places, in a way. The fox led me to you and showed me that being alone all the time isn't very helpful. And the hare showed me that things with Mum . . .' I trail off, licking my lips. 'It showed me that maybe I'm not *fine* all the time.'

Kwame keeps cycling, slowly.

'And the raven – the raven showed me your grandad and Joel needed help . . .'

'And it took you to the train line,' Kwame says.

I shake my head. 'That was just where Joel was . . .' But now I'm saying it, I'm not sure. A distant memory itches at the back of my mind and makes me hold onto Kwame a little tighter.

We ride onto our street in silence, only stopping when I see the curtains of my house all closed up tight.

'Do you want to come round my house?' Kwame asks. 'Friday night is barbecue night.'

It sounds nice, but all that busy already feels too much after what happened today.

'No, thanks, Kwame. Maybe next time.'

I climb off his bike and start to walk away, but he pulls me back into a big hug, his handlebars awkwardly digging into my ribs.

'I don't know about being brave for myself, but I'll always be brave for you, Nora Frost,' he whispers in my ear.

It's a weird-but-nice thing to say and I wiggle away, giving him a little wave as I put my helmet away. But I wait until he's gone round the bend before opening the front door.

For a moment, I dare myself to hope that Mum is up and making dinner and waiting for me. But the house is still and quiet and full of ghosts.

The note Kwame gave me is folded into the creases of my hand and I open it slowly.

Nora,

I'm sorry. Can you go round to Saffie's or Kwame's house?

I love you.

Mum x

I tiptoe up the stairs, feeling the knot in my belly tighten when I think about what the raven taught me today.

That maybe it's time to try and be brave for myself and let people help me – the same way I helped Kwame's grandad and Joel.

I put my hand on Mum's closed door. 'I'm sorry, too,' I whisper.

PART FOUR

THE OTTER

21

I wake up to something in my room and I think for a moment that the fox is back, sitting on my chest in the middle of the night.

Blinking, I squint at the rainbow shape that's frantically trying to get my attention by jumping up and down on me with his cold-nothing paws and skipping around my room in a circle.

I put my glasses on and see the rainbow blur is the ghost of an otter, his fur slick like he has just jumped out of the water and straight into my room.

I sit up and the otter shows his teeth in celebration of me *finally* being awake. I shake my head free of dreams and when I open my eyes again, the otter has been replaced by a shape like a giant grizzly ghost bear bending over my bed. I gasp, but there's no fuzzy rainbow halo or ghostly fur – just a big belly and a moustache.

'Bill,' I say, rubbing my eyes and still looking for the otter. 'What are you doing here?'

'Hey, kid,' Bill whispers. 'Your mum messaged me and so I've come over for a bit. She said you have a friend down the road – Kwame, is it?'

I nod, the words not really going in my head.

'Well, how do you feel like going for a little sleepover?'

I lean over to squint at my alarm clock. 'But it's 6 a.m.,' I say.

Bill stands up. 'It's okay – I called them and they're up with baby John anyway. Are you okay to get dressed?'

I nod and Bill leaves. I'm shaking as I put on my dungarees though and I put my T-shirt on inside out, because Bill has never been in my room before and something is wrong. I'm not sure what I need, so I pick up my school bag, even though it's Saturday. My notebook is still in there, hiding my terrible words like a guilty secret. I tiptoe out to see Bill bent in the doorway of Mum's room, saying something to her in a low voice.

I tap him on the shoulder and he smiles at me, closing the door.

'Is she okay?' I whisper.

'She's okay,' he says, his big hands on my shoulder. 'I think she just needs a bit of space today, if that's okay with you? And your mum would much rather you be with a friend – I know she always asks you to pop over someone's house in the notes she leaves.'

I nod guiltily, wondering if Mum knows I always ignore that part. I've always wanted to stay so I can help make her better, but I missed not going to Kwame's house for barbecue food last night.

Bill ushers me down the stairs.

'Can I say goodbye?' I ask.

'You can say hello tomorrow – how about that?'

Tomorrow feels like ages away, as it's not even properly today yet. But Bill waits for me as I put my shoes and coat on before we leave into the dawn, where the sky is bleeding into a new day.

I look back at the house as he leads me down the road.

'Do you have your dad's number at all, kiddo?'

I blink, surprised, as no one has ever asked me that

before. 'He doesn't have his own phone – he just calls me when he can from other people's.'

'And how about your grandparents, or aunties and uncles? Your mum's not mentioned them much over the years.'

I think about that, and the shape in the background of the photos on the kitchen table. And there's that nagging shadow of a memory somewhere in the back of my mind, too, like it's sitting at the bottom of the canal with my bike. Eventually though, I shake my head. 'It's just Mum and me – we're all we need . . .'

The old words feel strange when I say them now.

I look back at my house getting smaller and smaller.

When we get to Kwame's house, he's already looking out of the window, waiting for me in tiger-striped pyjamas that still have the label on. I stop and hold Bill's sleeve, looking up at him and his tired eyes and haywire hair. I want to ask him if everything is okay. I want him to tell me it's all *fine*.

Instead, he bends down and gives me a hug. 'I'm here for you and your mum any time, anywhere. You remember that, okay?'

He stands up and I nod. 'Are you going back to her now?'

'I am,' he says. 'I've got it from here, kiddo. Meanwhile, you have fun with Kwame, okay? Your mum – she'll be alright. Try not to worry.'

Kwame stands at his door in bare feet.

I look again at Bill, but he's already walking back up the hill to Mum. Kwame hops out, taking my backpack from me.

'Come on,' he says. 'Dad's making pancakes.'

I shrug off the tight feeling in my tummy as best as I can and follow him inside.

Breakfast at Kwame's house isn't like breakfast at mine, even on a Good Day. There's music playing from the radio on the windowsill whilst Kwame's dad sways left and right to it, singing out of tune. Baby John is wriggling around in his highchair, and Owen and Payne are sword fighting with their forks at the table.

'Nora!' Kwame's dad says when he sees me. 'So lovely to have you. What do you want on your pancakes?'

He plucks the fork-swords out of Owen's and Payne's hands and lays them flat on the table.

'Oh – um – whatever, really,' I say shyly.

'Have some Nutella!' Payne shouts.

'No, peanut butter and jam!' Owen shouts back.

'I have honey on mine,' Kwame says, sitting next to

me as his dad puts a huge stack of fluffy pancakes on the table.

'Honey sounds nice,' I say, and Kwame squirts some on my plate.

'Good choice, good choice,' his dad says, dancing to the song again.

The pancakes are good – the honey is sweet and makes my insides feel more settled – but I'm still secretly pleased when Kwame grabs my arm and pulls me up, saying, 'Come see my room.'

'What about the plates?' I ask, stumbling after him.

Kwame shrugs. 'Dad'll do them.'

It feels weird just leaving them sitting there, so I say thank you to his dad and clomp up the stairs after Kwame, nearly bumping into his mum coming out the bathroom with her hair wrapped up.

'Morning, Nora,' she says, as Kwame pulls me into his room.

Kwame's room isn't like mine – it's packed full of stuff from top to bottom, so you can hardly see the floor. The biggest thing in the room is a bunk bed – the top one with a sleeping shape still in it, and the bottom with a tiger-striped bedspread.

'Is someone up there?' I whisper to Kwame as he

jumps onto the bottom mattress.

'It's my older brother Izaak – he'll sleep in for ages on a Saturday. You don't have to be quiet though – Payne once jumped up and down on top of him for a full five minutes and he never woke up.'

I giggle as Kwame pulls out his notebook and scatters drawings of the fox, the hare and the raven until they cover the bed.

'I'm glad you're here – I wanted to see you today,' he says happily. 'I kept thinking about what you said about the raven and how it wanted you to go onto the railway line.'

I sigh, sitting so my back is against the wall. 'It's too dangerous to go down there, Kwame.'

'Only if you're on the tracks without a train,' he says, his finger in the air.

'But where are we going to get a train from?'

He leans over to the desk by his side, giving his brother on the top bunk a glance to see if he really is asleep, before taking a laptop out of the drawer with stickers across it that say DO NOT TOUCH and THAT MEANS YOU, KWAME.

'We get a train like everyone else does . . .' He types something into the laptop before swinging it around to face me. 'At the train station.'

He shows me a blue-and-white screen with a train drawing running along the top. In the first box, he's put the name of our local train station – the one in town that I've not been to for ages. But the bottom box marked 'Destination' is empty.

My insides flip. From under the bed, the ghostly shape of an otter comes skipping out, one paw up on the mattress and his head cocked to the side.

My heart thuds.

'We don't know that the raven wanted us to get on a train,' I whisper.

Kwame looks at me. 'I know, but . . . what do *you* think, Nora? Do *you* think we need to take a train somewhere?'

I mean to shake my head, but the otter jumps onto my lap and it comes out as a nod.

I look down, the otter staring at me wide-eyed and alert. It sees into the place in my mind I keep that lost memory of the train. And I know what he wants us to do.

'I don't know where we're going,' I whisper.

'For the "destination" bit?' Kwame asks, looking back at the laptop screen. 'It probably doesn't matter. We'll just get a ticket to a place that sounds interesting, then once we're through the ticket barriers, we can follow . . . the ghost animals . . . onto the train.'

The otter spins round in a circle like he thinks it's the best idea he's ever heard.

But it's a *bad* idea. It might be dangerous. And can we even go on a train on our own when we're ten years old?

Kwame looks at me and reaches for my hand. 'You told me to be brave for myself, Nora. This is me being brave. But maybe you need to be brave for yourself, too.'

I look at the drawings of the fox, the hare and the raven on Kwame's bed. I want to tell him I'm scared and that I don't want to. But also, I know deep down that this is the right thing to do – even if I'm not entirely sure why.

I just need to be brave enough to do it.

I give Kwame a small nod and he smiles in huge dimples as the otter runs excitedly out of the door.

22

The first part of Kwame's plan to follow the ghost animals involves getting away from our parents for the day. That turns out to be easy though, as Mum thinks I'm at Kwame's, and Kwame tells his mum that we're going to spend the whole day with his grandad, and she doesn't seem to mind.

'Take him some lunch now,' she says, handing Kwame a Tupperware box of curried potatoes whilst baby John gurgles in her ear and Owen and Payne wrestle on the floor at her feet.

We're breathless as we put our shoes and coats on, and I give my best innocent face as we leave, but no one really looks twice at us or notices at all.

'Do you think we'll get caught?' I say to Kwame.

He laughs. 'When you have as many brothers as I do, it's easy to disappear.'

We walk up the hill, and I look at his camouflage coat. 'You disappear a lot, don't you? Under the tree at school and to your grandad's caravan.'

Kwame looks at his feet. 'I suppose.'

I hold onto the other handlebar of his bike and help him push it up the hill. 'I see you, Kwame.'

He grins and stands a little taller.

I look at my red front door as we go past it to give Kwame's grandad his Tupperware of lunch and stay sat on the wall that encircles the house whilst Kwame makes us some cheese and pickle sandwiches to take with us. It's funny, because anyone looking at my house right now would think it was the same as it always is. But I notice all the curtains shut and Bill's car on the road outside and how quiet it is – like it's in the eye of a storm.

Kwame darts out of the house behind me and shakes a metal tin in my ear, making me jump.

'My life savings!' he says. 'I keep the tin in Grandad's caravan so Payne doesn't steal it.'

The coins rattle in the tin and it sounds like quite a lot.

'Weren't you saving to buy something special?' I ask.

He shakes his head but looks at his shoes. 'Nothing, really. This is more important.'

I'm not sure, but Kwame puts the tin in my bag and we hop on his bike, giving one last look at my house and his grandad's before we set off.

My insides are snaking and rumbling like we're riding over cobbles.

'Do you think the plan will work?' I ask Kwame.

'We won't know unless we try, will we?'

I nod and grip his sides tighter.

I'm not sure how to get to the train station from my house. I know it's in the middle of the town centre, but the only way we've ever gone there before is by car. But Kwame leads us down the canal path like he knows the way, and it feels nice to cycle back down here again. The sun is out today, waking bees who fly drunkenly into spring flowers, and glinting off the canal water like it's full of murky diamonds. It smells like new things and it loosens the nervous knot in my stomach.

When we get to the steep bank that the raven flew up yesterday, Kwame keeps cycling on – further than I've ever been down the canal before. I look into the water for the ghost of my bike on the bottom, but don't see it or any other ghosts either.

'Anything yet?' Kwame asks as if reading my mind.

I shake my head against his back.

The path narrows and we get off to walk single file for a while and give Kwame a break. Then, when we duck under a bridge and the path widens into one with a separate footpath and cycle path, I take over riding whilst Kwame sits on the back. It's hard to get going, even with Kwame giving us a push with his feet, and I'm laughing, which doesn't help.

'This is really hard!'

'Do you want me to take over again?'

'No, I can do it.'

Once we start moving, things get a bit easier. I can tell Kwame is thinking about how slow we're going though, and I should probably say sorry now for making fun of him all that time.

A rainbow flicker catches my eye ahead and I nearly topple us both into the canal.

'Nora, what—?' Kwame says as I stop the bike.

'Ghost otter!' I shout, pointing across the river to where he's bounding happily across the bank.

Kwame gasps. 'Of course! An Otter Adventure!'

I roll my eyes. 'Another one of your grandad's games?'

But Kwame shakes his head, grinning. 'This one's all ours, Nora Frost.' He fumbles for his notebook in his bag. 'What's it doing?'

The otter dives into the canal without even making a splash.

'Swimming,' I say, pointing onwards. 'That way.'

Kwame whoops. 'Then we're going the right way!'

I quickly try to push us off again, but it's difficult when I'm breathing so fast.

'Let me,' Kwame says.

I huff. 'I can do it—'

'I'm not saying you can't – it's just that—'

But I roar over his words and push down with all my weight to get us moving, so Kwame has to grab on tight.

The otter is fast in the water and doesn't look back, sticking out from the murky brown only because of his rainbow edges. When we have to go up and over a bridge, I think for a moment that we've lost him, but then he's there suddenly at our wheels, running alongside us, fur glinting in the sun.

I laugh loudly and wish Kwame could see him. Instead, I tell him about his many whiskers, webbed paws and long, pointed tail. Kwame tries to draw him in shaky pen, using my back as an easel.

The path widens and across the water is a pub called The Navigation, with benches outside and a family tucking into brunch. It makes me think strangely of Dad and how Bill asked me about him earlier, and so I nearly don't spot the otter suddenly freezing in my path. He's looking towards the canal boat tied onto metal stakes on the path next to us.

I wobble, putting my feet down and skidding into a bush of stinging nettles the other side of the path.

'Ouch!' Kwame says, rubbing at his ankles where the nettles caught the bit of his leg not covered by tiger-striped socks. 'What—?'

'Sorry,' I say. 'The otter stopped.'

A dog is madly barking from the boat as Kwame gets off the bike, still rubbing his ankles. The dog is small with a squished face and is yapping again and again like he's witnessed a terrible accident. I look over to the otter, who is now hiding in the long grass beside the boat, even though I don't think the dog can see him.

I drop the bike into the bush and walk over to the dog. The boat is green, with flowers painted across the side and the name *The Adventurer* between two gold windows, with curtains either side. The dog puts his paws on the edge as we get close, stopping barking to try and lick my hand as I reach out.

I laugh. 'You feel so warm compared to the ghosts!'

'We should get going,' Kwame says, standing behind me for some reason.

But then the door to the boat opens and a familiar lady's voice inside says, 'What's all the fuss?' And then out comes my teacher, Miss Omar.

I step back as Kwame steps forward.

'Nora?' she says, blinking, looking between Kwame and I. 'What are you doing here? What's wrong?'

I think of the notebook she gave me, hidden in my bag. 'Nothing's wrong,' I say, quickly. 'We're just out for a bike ride.'

'We're going to the train— Ouch!' Kwame says, as I step on his toe.

Miss Omar looks at us curiously before coming out onto the deck, the dog bounding over to her.

'It's okay, Fox,' she says, scratching the dog behind the ears. 'This is Nora from my class – not a burglar.'

'Fox?' I say, looking over to the otter, who's eyeing the dog moodily as he slips into the water again. 'Do you live here, Miss Omar?' I ask.

Miss Omar smiles, holding her cup of tea close to her chest. She looks strange in a navy headscarf and leggings and not the rainbow colours she normally wears in class.

'Sometimes,' she says. 'Sometimes I move the boat somewhere else and change the view.'

My mouth is hanging open, because I never thought

of anyone living in a boat before – especially my teacher.

'What kind of dog is Fox?' Kwame asks, sketching.

'He's a pug. Still a puppy, really, so he gets excited with new people.'

Fox the pug runs over to me, his claws scattering on the wooden deck of the boat. I put my hand out and stroke his short fur, giggling at how his skin gathers up on his back like a fat baby, and how his nose is squished into his face.

Kwame takes another step back behind me for some reason.

Miss Omar smiles. 'How are you getting on, Nora? Are you making use of that notebook I gave you? I'd love to read it sometime, if you're happy to share.'

I stop petting Fox and look at my feet. I can feel myself going red just thinking about anyone reading that awful line I wrote – the one Joel almost read out to the world. 'We can't stop today, we're—'

'We're on an adventure! Like your boat,' Kwame exclaims from behind me.

Miss Omar smiles warmly. 'Well, don't let me stop you. Although maybe think about adventuring close to home today, you two – there's a storm coming.'

We look up to the sky with her, but even though there

are racing clouds, it's blue with a bright morning sun.

'It was lovely to see you, Nora, and you too, Kwame. Do say hello if you ever pass the boat again.'

'You too,' I say as she and Fox disappear back inside the cabin.

I turn around and see Kwame drawing a storm in his notebook and I look again at the bright blue sky.

'Do you think we should go back?' I ask, nervously.

The otter gives a yelp-bark that sounds like it's from another planet, leaping out from the water to bound over to our bike, urgently.

Kwame shuts his book and picks up his bike from the stinging nettles. 'My grandad always says there's no such thing as bad weather – just bad clothing. And we've got our coats, haven't we?'

He puts his camouflage hood up, grinning at me, but stops when he sees me looking down the path towards home.

'If you're not sure, Nora, we don't have to go,' he says. 'It's okay if you want to turn back.'

I bite my lip. Part of me would like to go home, where it's safe. But something else inside me is urging me on, and it looks a little like a rainbow otter, trying to tug at my socks with his teeth.

'No,' I say, finally. 'Let's have that Otter Adventure.'

Kwame grins and clips his helmet on, jumping onto the front of the bike before I can argue, and we set off after the otter.

23

After what seems like a whole morning of riding along the canal and dodging runners and people walking with prams, the otter finally jumps out of the water and runs up a steep hill to a bridge. We get off and push the bike up between us, looking around.

We're on a small road at the back of a big brick building, and the otter bounds over to a bike rack that's already stacked up with all kinds of bikes.

I laugh. 'I think the otter wants us to drop the bike off, Kwame.'

Kwame looks excited as he runs the bike across the road carefully. 'Do you think animals get cleverer after they die?'

I frown whilst Kwame locks his bike along with our helmets, because even though the animals are ghosts, I've never really thought about them being dead before. It makes my heart beat that little bit faster as we both take a sip of the water he packed with the sandwiches.

'Do you know where we are?' I say, taking in our surroundings.

Kwame squints. 'I think so. It's this way.'

The otter follows us this time as Kwame heads towards a busy street with lots of people looking at their phones as they walk, somehow also knowing to dodge out of the way of each other. I look around at the shops and restaurants, and the Ferris wheel in the distance over the top of a big department store.

'Are we in town?' I ask Kwame, blinking.

'Yeah!' Kwame shouts over the noise of the street, his dimples out.

I can't believe we cycled all this way. Mum and I haven't been for ages – not since she was diagnosed. I know why, now I'm here – there are too many people and flashing lights and the roaring sound of trains, and my breath quickens like I'm feeling Mum's feelings for her.

Searching for the otter, I see him threading expertly through the legs of the people, none of whom pause to stop and stare or see anything. I'm less good at dodging and get shouted at by a lady in high heels when I bump into her.

'Watch where you're going!' she says, not looking at me at all.

'Sorry!' I call, but she's already clopped off, and Kwame follows her towards the large arched door of the train station.

The ceilings are high and the noise of shoes and announcements echoes around the foyer – a board of destinations flickering in the centre. It sort of looks familiar, but also much bigger and louder than I remember. I hold on to Kwame's arm as he digs around in my bag for his tin of money.

'Are you okay?' I ask him.

He grins at me. 'Sure! It's exciting, isn't it? I love trains. I wonder if we'll see a steam train, or if they'll all just be the modern ones? Maybe I'll ask when I buy our tickets.'

Kwame is being really brave and I do my best to act

like I am, too. I try to smile back at him, but I can feel it wobbling on my face. He walks me towards a queue of people waiting in a line separated by a black ribbon and I peer around for the rainbow edges of the otter.

'I can't see him,' I say nervously, holding on to Kwame's arm tighter.

He stops counting change to look with me, even though he wouldn't be able to see him anyway. The noise is loud and I can feel the eyes of the people looking at us, maybe wondering where our parents are. And I'm just wondering if I can ask Kwame if we can go home after all, when I see the swish of a tail slip under one of the black gates to the platforms.

'Hey!' I say, letting go of Kwame and ducking under the black ribbon. I push past someone with bright red hair who is carrying a suitcase and run towards the gates, bouncing off them when they don't open. The gates are black and rubbery, folded like the ones you see in Wild West films. I push them with all my might and they don't budge.

'You need a ticket,' the person with the suitcase says angrily from behind me.

I step back to let them through, looking around for the otter, but not seeing him on the platform.

I'm feeling lost and impossibly far from Mum, when I feel Kwame's hand on my shoulder.

'You forgot your ticket,' he says, handing me a strip of orange card. 'There aren't any steam trains apparently, so I just got us a ticket to the next station along. Shall we give it a go?'

I can't speak, so I grip his hand and follow him back towards the gates, watching him as his ticket is sucked into the machine at the gate and then popped out at the top. He takes it and the gate magically opens, letting him through. I sort of remember that, now I've seen it, and I follow him.

'Which train shall we get on?' Kwame asks, like I should know.

We get caught up in a crowd that pushes us towards a huge train that's chugging out exhaust fumes from hot vents in the side.

The people around us surge down the platform, looking at carriage numbers and counting them down over the whistle of the conductor.

'All aboard!' he shouts, waving a paddle with a reflective surface.

Kwame looks at me. 'Is it this train?' he shouts over the noise.

The conductor blows his whistle again and the last few passengers hurry up the big step onto the train. I chew on my cheek and think of Mum at home and wonder what I should do.

The signs on the side of the carriages flicker on, saying the train is destined for a place called South Otley. Suddenly, I see a rainbow haze at the window of the carriage in front. It's the otter, slick paws up on the glass. And I can see that he's yelping, telling us to *hurry up, hurry up!*

'Otter!' I shout.

The doors beep and start to close. I pull Kwame up the step and we just make it into the carriage before the door slams shut behind us.

My heart is thrumming in my ears. A little girl in a pushchair looks at us, our hands and knees on the floor, panting. The train fires up, sounding loud and strange, and we start to move.

Kwame helps me up, looking around us and down at his ticket. 'Do you know where South Otley is?' he asks me.

It sounds familiar, but I'm not sure why, so I shake my head. Instead, Kwame taps the lady holding the pushchair on the arm.

'Excuse me, can you tell us where we're going, please?'

The lady doesn't look like she understands, but the girl in the pushchair laughs and claps her hands.

'We're going to the sea!' she cries.

24

My insides feel like I'm already on the sea and they swish and swirl dangerously. Kwame sees and tries to steady me, but I shake him off, dusting myself down.

'We can't go to the sea,' I hiss. 'It's too far.'

Kwame bites his lip, looking nervous too for the first time since we left home. 'Well, we're on the train now, and it's not like we can get off. Why don't we try to find the otter and we'll make a plan.'

The carriage is full of families with bags packed for weekends away, children pointing at the disappearing

station behind us
from their parents'
laps. No one really
takes any notice of Kwame
and me as we walk between the
seats, swinging left and right as the train
rocks over the tracks. Halfway down, the carriage
lurches to the side and I stumble into a man's arm,
so he tuts at me.

'Sorry,' I say. 'It was the train.'

He doesn't look at me, but I wish he would. I wish
we'd get caught and sent back home before Mum
realizes we're missing. I stumble towards a set of
doors with a circular button, which I press to slide
them open.

In the elbow between carriages, the noise
is huge. I can hear the wheels of the train
clacking over the tracks and see the
town whooshing by the window
outside.

Kwame leans in from
behind me to press
another button and
the noise silences.

This carriage is emptier and only a few people are on seats, all listening to music through their headphones or typing on laptops. I look around for the otter's rainbow glow. And then, in a quiet part at the back of the carriage, I see him, curled on a seat and hugging his tail with his long clawed toes.

'There!' I say, feeling a rush of relief sweep over me.

I want to throw myself into the seat next to him, because seeing him again feels like finding myself. It feels nice to see him so calm, when before he's been so eager and desperate for me to follow him – like time is running out. It makes me feel calmer, too.

I sit in the seat opposite, so Kwame is near the window and I can keep an eye on the otter.

'I've never seen an otter before, have you? Before today, I mean,' Kwame adds quickly, getting out his journal and turning to the shaky drawing he did. 'I'd forgotten what they look like.'

'I feel like I've seen one once,' I say. 'But I can't remember where . . .'

The otter's long whiskers twitch as he stretches and tucks his pointed tail further under his chin.

'What's he doing?' Kwame asks.

'Just sleeping,' I whisper. 'Maybe he's tired.'

I'm feeling tired too, when suddenly, the train's horn blares out, making us both jump. Out the window, we see a rush of a steep slope, with familiar steps leading up to a wooden gate.

Kwame smiles, shakily. 'At least we know we're going the right way.'

I bite my lip again and Kwame takes a deep breath, pulling out the sandwiches he packed earlier.

'It can't be that far to the sea,' Kwame says. 'Grandad used to go there all the time in his caravan just for one night – just to see the ships on the horizon. We'll see where the otter takes us, have an adventure and hop on the train back in time for tea.'

He seems like he's trying to convince himself as well as me. I can't help but think of Mum and how nervous she was when I disappeared that time I lost my bike. But then, she thinks I'm at Kwame's all day anyway, doesn't she? And Bill says she needs her space.

Kwame takes a bite out of his sandwich and sprays crumbs over me when he talks. 'Have you been to the sea before?'

I frown, nodding. 'I think so . . . With my mum . . . and my dad.'

He stops trying to talk and it feels like he's giving

me a blank page to write on, so I sigh and tell him the story.

'I'm not very good at remembering that far back, because I haven't seen Dad since he and Mum got divorced. But I know he wore a gold ring that had the letter "D" on it. That stood for his name – Derek. And I remember being with him and Mum in a boat on the sea, rocking back and forth.'

The train rocks from side to side and it's like I'm there again, listening to the seagulls squawking and smelling doughnuts and feeling grains of sand between my toes.

'I remember being in a boat with a motor and the waves slapping the bottom. And the taste of the salt in my hair as it whipped into my mouth. Mostly though, I remember the shouting.'

'Like Joel's mum and dad?' Kwame asks.

I shrug. 'I guess. Mum was shouting that Dad was going too fast, and Dad was laughing with his head back, making the boat jump and smash through the waves even more, jerking us left, right and all over. It was exciting, but also it hurt when the side of the boat knocked into my bones.

'Dad is a wild adventurer. And he wanted to take us along for the ride, but I suppose it was too fast and dangerous for Mum. She stood up and leaned over to switch off the engine herself, when a wave jumped up like a whale, knocking into the bottom of the boat, and she fell overboard.'

'Oh no!' Kwame says, his eyebrows raised.

'I was shouting, but Dad just laughed. I don't think Mum found it very funny though. She was quiet when Dad pulled her back into the boat, and quiet all the rest of the day. In fact, I don't really remember her saying anything at all until she was sitting with me on my bed and telling me that Dad had moved out.'

Kwame tries to hold my hand, but I move it and pretend I didn't notice.

'It's okay though. Dad got his dream job saving tigers in India. And Mum and I are *fine* . . .'

I trail off, because that word doesn't feel right any more – not since everything the ghost animals have taught me. It also feels like there is more to the story, but it's all murky and I can't remember.

Kwame starts talking about all the times he's been to the beach with his family, but looking at the otter sleeping, I remember how tired I am too and close my eyes. I must doze off, because it's some time later when a shout wakes me with a start.

'Tickets, please!'

Kwame grabs my arm, his eyes wide as a lady with her hair tied in a neat bun and dressed in the same material as the seats on the train makes her way down the aisle towards us, checking people's tickets.

'We don't have the right ones!' he hisses. 'We'll get caught.'

My stomach flips and I look at the otter, now fully awake and on the floor of the carriage, his wet fur on end.

'Come on,' I whisper, dragging Kwame off the seat.

The otter follows at our feet to the door at the other end, the noise from the train loud again when I press the button.

'What do we do?' Kwame shouts over the sound of the tracks rumbling. 'We can't outrun her – there's not enough train!'

The otter looks frozen and scared, paws out in front of him, eyes looking from left to right for a hiding place that will fit an otter and two human children. And I recognize him like I'm looking into a strange mirror.

I hear a click and a lady comes suddenly out from a door next to us, almost as surprised to see us as we are her.

'Oh, sorry, dear,' she says, her glasses falling from her nose and her handbag swinging out at me from the doorway. 'Were you waiting long?'

She holds the door open for me, looking strangely at Kwame by my side, and inside is a bad smell and a floor covered in toilet roll.

'Tickets, please!' I hear from the carriage behind us – the conductor now just behind the glass.

'Thank you!' I say to the lady, diving round her handbag and dragging Kwame into the toilet cubicle with the otter. We lock the door with a snap, just as we hear the conductor outside, asking the lady for her ticket.

I let out a sigh of relief as Kwame gags.

'This smells horrible!' he says.

I shush him, but he's right. The otter keeps his paws tucked close in the small space of floor that isn't covered in tissue or what I hope is water. He doesn't look too pleased to be stuck here with us, and I roll my eyes.

'Well, you didn't need to come in,' I say. 'She wouldn't have been able to see you, anyway!'

Kwame starts laughing, and maybe it's because the toilet is small and wobbly and smells so bad, but I start laughing too, my hand over my mouth.

'We have to stay quiet; she might hear us,' I whisper.

We try to listen out for the conductor on the other side of the door, but it's loud on this part of the train and I can only hear voices, not what they're saying. Kwame washes his hands in the sink whilst we're here and I look at our greenish faces in the cracked mirror.

'Do you think we'll be trapped in this toilet for the whole rest of the journey?' he says, drying his hands.

The otter doesn't look too thrilled about that and makes a high, angry yapping noise. Thankfully though, the train starts to slow down soon after and we hear someone speaking over the tannoy outside.

'*We will shortly be arriving at South Otley, our final destination. Please ensure you have all your belongings with you before exiting the train.*'

Kwame clutches me, his eyes bright and excited again. 'We're here! The sea!'

The train stops and I open the toilet door a crack to check that the coast is clear before we quickly jump the step off the train onto the platform. We whoop and cheer, the wind in our smiles as we run along the platform, following everyone down the stairs to the exit.

The weather has turned since we left home – the blue

sky ahead is now a purplish-grey. There's a cold wind and the fizz of something too, like the feeling you get when you're on the top of the diving board, about to jump off into the pool.

Kwame looks up. 'Maybe Miss Omar was right, after all – there might be a storm coming.'

When we get to the bottom of the stairs though, we have bigger things to worry about. Six huge black gates, like the ones at the station before.

Kwame pulls back. 'Our tickets won't work in those; we don't have the right ones.'

The otter runs on ahead, his long body winding between suitcases and shoes.

'Come on!' I say, dragging Kwame with me behind a large group of people, all wearing the same purple T-shirts and singing songs. Their elbows jostle us as they dance, and I lose Kwame for a moment in the bodies. I hear the man on the gates laugh and the beep of an extra-large disabled gate open, before a cheer erupts from the people around us. And Kwame and I are taken through the open gate on the wave, our smiles wide.

I find him again at the doors, his shoulders back and face beaming. 'We did it!'

He seems taller somehow, and I nudge him as I spot the otter disappearing down a strangely familiar row of steps up ahead.

'Come on!' I shout.

We run across the station courtyard and down the steps, which go on and on past houses and shops selling fishing nets, which sway in the wind. The otter weaves left and right down the stairs like he's dancing, and I feel like dancing too, because we made it safely to the sea and it feels strangely like coming home.

When we get to the bottom, we cross a busy road at the traffic lights and scramble round a tall wire fence to a dockyard where boats of all kinds are raised up on giant stilts, painted all the colours of a ghost.

The otter weaves under them and we duck under the hulls of big yachts and sailing ships until the concrete floor disappears and a grey, murky sea stretches from the harbour to a small island with angry waves crashing against rocks.

It smells like old fish and salt and it feels so familiar. The otter looks round at me once, before diving into the water and disappearing in a rainbow ribbon.

'He's gone!' I say, running to the edge where water slurps and slaps against thick ropes on the side. We peer down and Kwame points out flashes of small fish near the bottom of the shallow water.

I look out to the sea, which chops left and right like it's boiling. The wind is much stronger here, and the clouds much darker, too, making the island on the other side of the harbour look like a dark, looming shadow. I feel something flicker in my memory as I raise my hand to point to the rocks in the distance, where waves froth white.

'I think he wants us to follow him there.'

Kwame spins round, looking between the sea and the darkening sky. 'Are you sure . . . ?'

I nod and Kwame sucks in a huge breath, puffing out his chest like a gorilla. 'Okay then, Nora Frost.'

He runs over to a wooden jetty with rotting planks and points over the edge. 'Look!'

There's a small boat with an engine on the back bobbing on the waves, just like the one I remember being in with Mum and Dad once upon a time. It's painted the same red as our front door, and on the side is a name.

'*The Adventurer,*' Kwame says. 'Just like Miss Omar's boat.'

It feels like a sign, but still I hesitate as Kwame jumps down into it, wobbling on the waves.

'Isn't it stealing, to take a boat?' I say.

Kwame moves the coils of ropes from the seats. 'We'll bring it back, won't we?'

It feels odd for Kwame to be so brave like this when I'm feeling so unsure. Above us, the clouds seem to darken and rumble.

'Why are you making me do this?' I whisper, my hands now in my pockets.

Kwame's eyebrows shoot up. 'I'm not making you do anything! You're the one that led us all the way here—'

'No I'm not!' I snap, as the wind whips up in a howl.

Kwame climbs back out of the boat, scrambling on the floor until he's stood back on dry land with me.

'You said you needed to get on a train, so—'

'No,' I say again, my fists clenching. 'The ghost raven showed me the train line. And the otter showed us the way to the train.'

A spot of rain falls from the sky and lands on Kwame's forehead and he wipes it away, quickly. 'Nora,' he sighs, before stopping himself. 'You remind me so much of my grandad sometimes.'

It's not at all what I expected him to say. I take a step back. 'What do you mean?'

'He's so stubborn about asking for help too. But – it's okay, Nora. Look, we've come all this way. I've been braver today than I ever have in my whole life and it's all down to you. And now, we just have one more thing to be brave for.'

He turns and jumps into the boat again, his hand out towards me. 'Come on, Nora – be brave for yourself.'

His words are ringing in my ears. I want to scream and shout that I'm nothing like his grandad and that I don't need help. But the sky rumbles somewhere far away and the ghostly face of an otter peeks from the growing waves.

Kwame is right. I've come this far. I just need to be brave enough to see the truth for myself.

I take a deep breath and climb into the boat without needing his hand, sitting at the front.

'Do you know how to—?'

But my words are swept away as Kwame yanks a long cord on the motor and it roars to life.

'Are you ready?' he shouts at me.

I look out towards the horizon. I don't feel ready, but then I look down and see flashes of rainbow otter fur under the waves, swimming right towards the island.

I know that the island is important, even if I can't

remember why. And even though I don't feel sure, or certain, or very brave at all – I have Kwame. And with a friend like him by my side, maybe I can finally be strong enough to make Mum proud.

'Let's go!' I shout over the motor, and Kwame throws off the rope tying us to dry land.

25

The waves in the harbour are small and easy for the little boat to cut through. But once we get out of the safety of the harbour wall and into the stretch of the sea, the waves become steadily bigger and bigger, until we're rising and falling like we're chopping up and down the back of a huge sea monster.

I grip the side of the boat so tightly, my hands turn blue. I feel the cold needle in through my dungarees and grit my teeth, turning back to check on Kwame, who looks just as cold and unsure as me now.

'Maybe we should turn back?' I shout over the roar of the motor and the water.

But Kwame's hands are tight on the rudder. 'It's not far – we just need to hold on!'

Holding on is easier said than done as the sky flashes above us like lights in a haunted house, rumbling a low thunder that sounds like a sea witch waking up. The spray from the sea splashes over the boat and more drops of rain fall from the sky, puddling on my glasses and turning everything splotchy. I squint out as the boat is tipped left and right, looking into the water for the otter, seeing nothing now but waves and clots of seaweed.

We've come a long way from the harbour, which sits between long stretches of pebble beaches and murky hotel buildings disappearing into the mist. It feels like we're leaving everything safe behind us and I can see in Kwame's eyes that he's feeling scared too.

The sky cracks with a fork of lightning, and a clap of thunder follows just after, which must mean it's right above our heads now.

'We've got to stay safe!' I shout into the wind.

The island is close enough now to see the waves lashing against the rocks and another boat tied onto a jetty ducking and swaying in the water. The waves toss us like we're in a washing machine and the engine struggles to power through them. And I'm just wondering if there are any life vests hidden under our wooden seats, when I spot a rainbow shimmer bobbing in the waves ahead.

I wipe my glasses and squint into the rain as we get closer. It looks like a rainbow rock with eyes, watching us.

'Ghost otter!' I shout to Kwame, my insides lighting up.

Kwame looks cold and scared, and so I shift back to sit with him, my hand over his on the motor and turning it up to full blast, so the little boat roars up and over a huge wave.

The otter dives and reappears by the boat, weaving around us like he's helping carve a path through the waves. I see a flash of whiskers and tail as he surfaces, before bobbing back below again.

'We're going to make it!' I say to Kwame, who narrows his eyes in the rain.

We point the boat at the jetty, and the waves send us much quicker than we thought towards it, so the boat smashes against the wood, splintering it. I stumble forward and Kwame cuts the engine, so the only sound is the roar of the sea and the rain spattering on the rocks. I can't see at all now, so I take off my glasses and dive blindly for the jetty, scrambling for a rope on the side to tie the boat to. I pass it to Kwame and he launches himself off the boat with me, panting.

I look back at the blurry line of the shore a whole mile away and see lights twinkling like stars.

'Come on!' I shout to Kwame, helping him up. 'We need to find somewhere dry!'

We stumble up and I put my glasses back on, although I can't see anything but raindrops. At my feet though, I see a rainbow glimmer of the otter ecstatically circling round us.

It's the right place and we're here and I wish I could feel glad, but instead I feel cold and scared. We climb a steep path together towards a tall house hidden from the shoreline by thick bushes and trees. And all around it are huge cages and sheds, with yellow eyes peering out at us as we climb the steps to a big red front door.

I think for a moment that I must know this door, but it's the same red as ours at home, so that's probably why. But I still pause before I knock on it.

'Go on – it's freezing!' Kwame says, blinking the rain out of his eyes.

'What if . . . what if it changes things?' I say, quietly.

The ghost otter looks at me and I know it sees my fear.

I can see all the questions in Kwame's eyes, but he doesn't get to ask them, as the door to the house opens suddenly, and there – looking down at us with a one-legged seagull in her arms – is an old lady.

And she looks very, very cross.

'What on earth do you think you're doing?' she shouts, as a clap of thunder makes Kwame and I jump.

I step back, looking at the blurry figure of the woman with the huge mess of grey hair towered on her head and wearing a patchwork dress. But she leans forward, grabbing the front of my dungarees, and pulls me inside with Kwame in tow.

The heat from her house immediately turns all the water on my glasses into steam, so I can just feel the squelch of water in my shoes and smell something sharp mixed with something sweet. Kwame is shakily apologizing, but he's shivering too much to make any sense, so the old lady sighs loudly.

'Goodness me – no – stay there. Stay!'

She barks at us like we're dogs, but we stay on the doormat whilst she disappears with the seagull. I take my glasses off and wipe them on my T-shirt before putting them back on again, squinting through the smudges at Kwame, who has a drip of rain hanging from his nose.

'Are you okay?' I whisper.

He nods and shivers, trying to take his shoes off without stepping off the mat.

'No – don't worry about those – come in here now. Come!'

The old lady barks at us like animals again, but we follow her anyway, away from the big hallway and into a large kitchen with a beamed ceiling.

Only it's not a kitchen. Not really.

There's a fridge in the corner with an owl sat on the top of it, his head cocked to the side and huge eyes on us. There's a worktop going round the outside with a huge snake slithering across it, his head resting in the fruit bowl. And there's a dog bed in the corner with what looks like a squirrel sleeping in it.

'Trespassing! In a storm, no less!' the old lady says, putting the one-legged seagull down next to the toaster and filling up the kettle from a sink with a huge toad sitting in it. 'Dangerous. Rude. Why, I have a good mind to throw you both out on your ears to look after yourselves!'

But she doesn't do that. Instead, she goes to a cupboard full of pet food and takes two towels from a sealed tub, thrusting them at us and nearly knocking Kwame over.

'Never in all my time . . .' she mutters.

The kettle squeals and the owl on the fridge joins it, setting off the parrot I'd missed that's sitting on the kitchen door, who meows like a cat.

The lady pours tea into two huge mugs, shaking her head so strands of silver hair fall out of her messy bun. Now I can see better, I can see her clothes are made up of lots of other types of clothes, all sewn together. I can see a whole baby's cardigan on the side under her left armpit.

'Sorry,' I mutter, but she doesn't really seem to be listening. I wring my hair out on the towel and Kwame gives me a terrified look.

'Is this the right place?' he whispers, looking around at all the animals.

I frown, unsure of what he means. I can't see any ghost animals leading the way any more. All these animals are alive, apart from the dead chicks in the fridge, which the old lady feeds to the owl above her before taking out a large, beautiful sponge cake.

'Well, sit down then!' she barks.

We look towards a kitchen table mainly made up of a huge tank with a giant spider in it. Kwame doesn't look sure about sitting next to it, but I pick my way across and make him follow.

The lady somehow balances the cake, the tea and the seagull in her arms, clucking at the animals as she moves towards the table, where she lays everything out and finally sits down.

'So,' she says, taking a huge knife out of her pocket and cutting up the cake. 'What, might I ask, are you doing on my island?'

I look at Kwame for help, but he's preoccupied with the spider in the tank.

'Why do you have all these animals?' I ask instead as the old lady slides two huge chunks of creamy cake across the table to us.

'All strays,' she says, waving her hand like feeding cake to a seagull in her lap is completely normal. 'Some injured, some lost. Some pets that never should have been pets. If an animal needs my help, then everyone knows old Nell is here to give it.'

The bird squawks in her lap.

'Even seagulls?' I say, looking at its huge beak and mean eyes.

She huffs, taking a bite from the bit of cake she just fed to the bird. 'All animals deserve help – especially the ones people seem to like less, for some reason.'

The squirrel I saw before wakes up, running across the kitchen to climb up my arm, its tiny claws clutching my still-wet hair.

'What's his name?' I ask, looking across at Kwame, who looks horrified. I suppose it is a little odd that all these animals are in the kitchen of a house in the middle of an island. Somehow though, it feels strangely like home.

Nell huffs again. 'He's a wild animal. Wild animals don't have names.'

The squirrel doesn't seem very wild. He rummages around in my hair before running back down my arm and over to Kwame, who leaps from the table.

'What's wrong?' I ask, as Kwame scratches himself, spinning in a circle.

'Nothing,' he says, but it doesn't look like nothing. It looks like he's panicking more now than we were in the boat.

'Not a fan of animals, hey?' Nell says, feeding a strawberry from the cake to the squirrel.

I glare at Kwame, my mouth open. 'What?! But – but

the hare. And the otter. And the others . . . ?'

Kwame shuffles from foot to foot, looking embarrassed. 'Yes, but I couldn't see them, could I?' he whispers.

I look at Nell to see if she heard that, but she's still feeding cake to the squirrel.

I remember now though how Kwame reacted to Fox the dog on the boat, and how he hid behind me.

'But you followed me all this time . . .' I say, as he ducks when the meowing parrot takes flight over his head, flapping to the other side of the kitchen.

'I thought it was just a game at first,' he mumbles. 'It wasn't until you told me what all the animals were teaching you that I finally understood. The animals aren't real, are they, Nora? They were just your way of asking for help.'

I feel a hot ball of anger in my throat and I turn away from him, my fists on the table.

All this time, I thought he believed me. But he didn't – just like everyone else. And his words feel complicated and knotted in my chest and that's not what real friends do to the people they care about.

I want to shout at him to go, but Nell passes his cake up to him with a kindness in her eyes that I haven't seen since we got here. 'Down the hall to the left is my study. There's a wildcat in there, but she's stuffed, so she shouldn't be any bother.'

Kwame looks unsure, but the owl gives another screech and he scarpers off, leaving me and Nell alone with the animals in the kitchen.

'Right,' she says, putting the squirrel back in his bed and looking fixedly at me. 'Are you going to tell me what you're doing here, then?'

I pick at my cake. It's one of those Victoria sponges that I used to make with Mum, with thick cream and strawberry jam.

Nell studies me. 'I know you're mad at your friend, but everyone is afraid of something, you know. Animals happen to be a common one, although I can't say I share it.' She strokes the seagull's head, who closes her eyes. 'And you – you're afraid of talking to me for some reason.'

'No I'm not,' I snap. She raises an eyebrow and I sigh. 'It's just complicated. You wouldn't understand.'

'Try me,' she says, putting the seagull down on a pile of tea towels on the bench next to her.

I lick my lips. It feels like I'm back around the breakfast table with Mum again, ghosts haunting my lips. But Kwame's words have got me feeling cross and confused, and I wonder if speaking out loud might help untie the knots in my chest.

'I've been seeing . . . animals. They've been visiting me. We followed them here.'

Nell's expression stays straight. She's got thick eyebrows and big eyes and seems very clean for a person covered in animals all the time.

'What kind of animals?'

I knock my wet shoes together under the table. 'A fox. A hare. A raven. An otter . . .'

Just then, we hear a thump from down the hall and the meowing parrot takes flight, flapping blues and reds round our heads as Kwame bursts into the room.

'Nora!' he says. 'You have to see!'

He beckons me out of the kitchen, down a hall and into a quiet, dark study cluttered with old furniture and photographs in frames.

'Look,' he says, excitedly, jumping over a desk full of paper and pointing at the pictures on the wall. 'A fox. A hare. A—'

'Tiger,' I say, gawping at the giant stuffed cat crouched in the corner, her yellow eyes piercing and her teeth bared.

Kwame frowns at me. 'But you didn't tell me you saw a tiger?'

I did though. Long ago – the stripes jumping off Dad's packed suitcase and becoming the ghost I'm seeing right here in Nell's study. It's like seeing her again, but rather than rainbow edges, she's frozen strangely in a dark, dusty room.

Kwame is almost hyperventilating, and I realize that I'm not breathing at all. I run over to him and see all the animals on the wall, and he's right. There they are – my fox and hare. And in other photos, the otter, the raven. And dozens of other animals I can remember seeing glints of – when I was angry when Dad first left, or scared of jumping into the swimming pool in Year Two . . .

Only they're not ghosts in the photos – they're alive.

I spin round as we hear a shuffle behind me, and Nell enters the room, looking at us, strangely.

'It's them,' I say, looking round the room. 'But why would they lead us here, to you?'

Nell looks confused, like she has no idea what I'm talking about. But Kwame rips a page out of his journal, scribbling something down.

'We did it, Nora – we finally found the answer. We finally know why we came all this way here, to this island, in the middle of a storm.'

He hands me the page, along with a large gold ring with a 'D' on it.

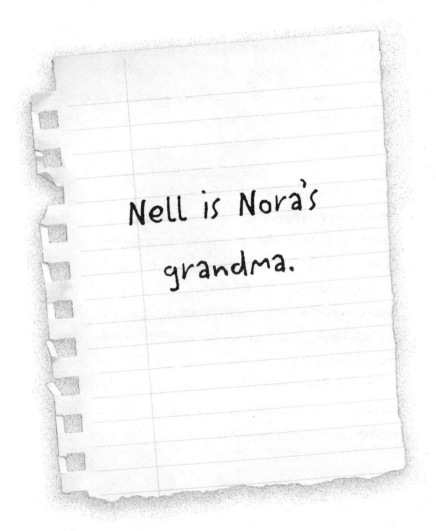

Nell is Nora's grandma.

26

My heart is hammering in time to the fat drops of rain on the diamond-leaded windows. Outside, the wind howls, and somewhere, an animal matches it.

'My grandma . . .' I whisper, looking at the woman with the patchwork clothes and the seagull.

Nell frowns, looking hard at me. 'You're . . . Nora? Miri's Nora?' She looks me up and down and then over to the broken clock on the wall for some reason. 'But you're only little, aren't you? Wait . . .' She counts something on her hands, all the way to ten and then blinks at me. 'Oh . . .'

My thoughts are racing like a flock of birds. I look at the ring Kwame gave me – the one I remember my dad wearing. 'Why do you have this?' I ask, my words somehow coming out angry.

'My son – your dad. He gave it to me to keep safe before he went away years ago. He wanted me to post it to him last year, but I told him that if he wanted it so badly, he was to come home and see—'

She looks at me and I feel my face heat up.

Nell is my dad's mum. My grandma. I shake my head, looking around. 'I don't remember . . . Mum never . . .'

But then I remember the blurry shape in the back of the photographs and the memory buried deep in my mind comes surging up like sunken treasure.

My grandma. Holding mine and Dad's hands as we raced around the island, a fox at my feet as a hare scarpered away, a raven called overhead and an otter disappeared into the sea.

Nell takes a step towards me, but I stumble back, so my shoulder hits the pictures on the wall.

'Well, you wouldn't remember,' she says. 'You've not been here since you were, what – five? And what a day that was – barely off the train when your mum fell out the boat, both of them squabbling like parakeets before your dad packed his bags. I hardly got a look at you before you were whisked away.'

I look at the stuffed tiger, her stripes matching my socks. 'But Mum never talks about you . . . Why haven't I seen you?'

Nell finally breaks her stare to straighten some of the pictures on the wall, her back to me. 'Well – your mum wasn't my biggest fan after your dad left. It was my idea he go to India, you see – he'd always wanted to go since we rescued Ethel when he was a boy.' She nods towards the tiger, sadly. 'He wanted to help – to make sure that no more tigers ever had to be rescued. I never dreamed that he wouldn't come back . . .'

'You could have called though,' I say, my voice small.

Nell folds her arms. 'Your mum made it perfectly clear that she was just *fine* on her own and that I wasn't needed. And I wasn't about to go grovelling any more than I already had – I know when I'm not wanted.'

My ears are burning and Kwame tugs on my hand. 'You should tell her,' he whispers. 'About your mum.'

I pull my arm away from Kwame and give him an angry stare as Nell whips round. 'What about your mum?' She looks between us. 'Has something happened? Is that why you're here?'

'We're *fine*,' I snap, marching round the desk to the door. 'Mum's right – we don't need anyone. This was a mistake.'

'But, Nora,' Kwame says, stumbling after me, 'the ghosts you've been seeing – what if they're not ghosts at all? What if all along they've just been hidden memories, or a part of you that knew you needed help and that your grandma is really good at giving it—'

'We don't need any help!' I shout, spinning on the spot so Kwame cowers away from my voice. 'The ghost animals are real and not one of your stupid games, or something I made up.' I turn to Nell, now looking for something in a cupboard. 'I'm going home.'

'Oh no you're not,' Nell says, digging an old-style phone out of the clutter with a long, coiled wire and plugging it into the socket on the wall. 'There's a storm. You'll drown before you've even left the island.'

She dials a number, but the hot anger is back and I don't want to be here. I pull open the door and stomp out to the hall. In the study, I hear Nell talking to someone on the phone and Kwame clattering after me. I quickly unlatch the door and it swings back on a huge gust of wind, setting all the animals yelping in the kitchen.

I grit my teeth and push myself outside, rain lashing at my cheeks like needles. Behind me, Kwame calls me back, but I pull my hair out of my face and march through the trees, where *The Adventurer* is bucking and swaying on the waves like a wild horse.

'Come back!' Kwame says, his words whipping away in the storm.

'Leave me alone!' I shout back. 'I'm *fine* by myself.'

I should never have let Kwame in. Mum and I are all we need – we don't need a grandma or friends or animal ghosts or memories. We're not strays and we're not broken – we have each other and that's all that matters.

The ghost animals were wrong to bring me here.

My hands are numb as I try to undo the thick rope tying the boat to the jetty. The waves are crashing against the rocks all around us – higher now than they were even just an hour ago. The wind is ferocious and I'm afraid, but I'm also angry and I can't see and all I know is that I need to get away.

I jump into the boat, falling forward as the waves rock it left to right. My hands are too cold to undo the neat double knot Kwame used to tie the boat up, and I yell in frustration.

'Nora, wait!' Kwame shouts, trying to climb down into the boat with me. 'It's dangerous.'

'Go away!' I shout at him. 'I'm *fine* on my ow—'

Just then, a huge wave crashes into the boat, smashing it into the jetty and sending splinters raining down on us. I fall on my hands and knees and taste blood on my tongue. But when I look up to the dark, bruised sky, I don't see Kwame anywhere.

My heart lurches and I spin round, stumbling in the boat. 'Kwame? Kwame!' I shout over the roar of the wind.

My glasses are blurred and I take them off again, squinting into the lashing rain for his camouflage coat. And then I see it – just a cuff, disappearing over the side of the boat.

'No!' I shout, diving towards it. My fingertips grab hold of his, just below the surface of the water. I pull with all my might and for a moment his face appears, gasping and scared, before another wave swallows him up.

The water is trying to take something from me again, but this time it's not a bike – it's a friend – and that's more precious than anything in the whole world. The boat rocks again, but it's not a wave this time – it's a person, who puts their hands over mine – like Kwame's did when I had my fingertips on the bike. They grab Kwame's wrist with me and I look up to see Nell's determined face.

'Let me help!' she shouts.

The ghost otter appears behind her and I don't push her off. Not for this.

Not for Kwame.

Together, we pull with all our might as more and more camouflage coat appears from the waves. Kwame splutters and gasps again as his face breaks the water, and he clutches the side of the boat as we heave him in with us.

It's a relief to see him slide into the boat, but we're not out of danger yet. Nell stands with perfect balance, hoisting Kwame onto the jetty whilst I push him from below. And then she lifts me up after him and the solid wood under our feet feels like taking a breath.

'I'm sorry, I'm sorry,' I say over and over to Kwame.

He tries to smile at me, but he's still shivering and

coughing seawater.

Nell picks him up and I put his arm over my shoulder. I put my water-blurred glasses back on and together, we walk him back towards the house.

27

Nell and I take Kwame up the rickety stairs in her house, being careful not to step on the animal cages piled up alongside the banister. Kwame is shivering a lot, so Nell transfers the catfish swimming around the bath into a big tub and runs Kwame a hot bath instead.

'We'll be outside,' Nell says, closing the door so Kwame is alone without any animals at all.

I'm shivering too – feeling awful for what I said to Kwame. Nell beckons me into a bedroom covered in pictures of elephants, with a tiger-striped spread on the large bed.

I run my hand along the stripes, looking round the room. 'Was this my dad's bedroom?'

'It was,' she says, taking out some old socks and trousers from the drawers. 'It was you and your mum's for a while too, you know. Your parents met so young and it all felt very rushed. And then your mum whisked you off to the mainland, and it was just me alone.'

A crow I hadn't spotted on the wardrobe flaps down and lands on her shoulder and she gives him a stroke.

'Is that why you got the animals? Because you were lonely?'

'I didn't get the animals, Nora – they found me. I've always had all this room on this island all to myself going to waste, so of course they could stay. Even when your dad was a boy and our animals were exotic circus rescues with nowhere else to go . . .'

I think about the tiger downstairs as I chew my lip, my heart still beating fast. 'They found me too – the animals.'

Nell doesn't stop rummaging through the drawers, but I think she's only doing it now so she's not looking at me, and I'm pleased.

'The fox. The hare. The raven and the otter. And even the tiger, one time . . .'

Nell stands and turns quickly. 'Ethel?'

I can't stop my smile. 'I thought they were wild animals and didn't have names.'

'Yes, well,' she says, shutting a drawer. 'She came pre-named from the circus. Plus, she was . . . special.'

She sits down on the bed, stroking the tiger stripes. I sit down next to her, picking at the scabs already forming on my hand.

'They *are* ghosts, you know. Not a game or a memory I made up, like Kwame said.'

I growl the last few words and Nell sighs, leaning over to touch my hand. 'It doesn't matter what they are, Nora. Sometimes we just see the things we need to see. There are some things we want to ignore because we don't want them to be true. But the world has ways to make us understand what needs to be done. It doesn't matter whether they're ghosts, or your own memories. When you think about it, they're probably the same thing, aren't they?'

The wind roars outside. I hadn't thought about it like that. Mum's got her own ghosts too – they're not animals like mine, but they are memories – haunting her every day. And I've always wanted to do everything I can to make them go away and stop people from seeing just how real they can be.

But maybe it's time to stop pretending now. Just because I want it to be true that I can make Mum better all by myself, doesn't mean that I can.

Nell pats my hand. 'I've been having dreams about a boat coming to my island for weeks, you know. It's been strange, because no one ever comes here. It's treacherous, plus there isn't much reason for anyone to come unless they're bringing me an animal – and no one has brought one of those to me for a while now. The laws have changed a lot since we rescued Ethel – thank goodness.

'But I had this feeling somehow that it was true. And even though I've been telling myself for years that I'm absolutely *fine* on my own here and everything is dandy, I found myself making cakes and waiting at the door for a knock, hoping . . .'

The crow on her shoulder caws and pecks strands from the bun on her head.

I bite my lips closed as the rain lashing on the window starts to slow to a light patter.

'Mum says we're *fine* too,' I whisper.

'And what do you think, Nora?'

I think of my journal in my school bag downstairs and the terrible words I wrote down. And I think of Nell's hands helping me heave Kwame out of the water and saving his life.

'I want to be as strong as her . . .' I say.

Nell bends over and hoists up a big book from under the bed, turning the pages until she finds one on ants.

'Ever seen an ant?'

I nod slowly, not sure if she's been listening.

'They're small but strong. They can carry up to twenty times their body weight all on their own. But they're also smart enough to know that one ant all by itself doesn't stand a chance. In groups, they can use their strength to lift impossible things and keep each other alive. It's marvellous, really.'

I trace my finger across the photo of the ant. 'I don't understand.'

'It's taken me a long time, too,' she says. 'But getting help – working together – it doesn't mean you're weak, Nora. If anything, it means the opposite.'

I look at her. She doesn't look like me, or maybe she does, in a strange way I can't see. But I feel like she – just like the ghost animals – understands me more than anyone else.

I bite my lip, looking around for the ghost otter to show me the way, but not finding him.

But I know what I need to do now. I just have to be brave enough to do it.

I look at Nell. 'I have a book too . . . Can I fetch it?'

She nods, stroking the crow, and I jump off the bed, going downstairs to the hallway where my bag is still sitting on the doormat. I reach inside and hold the raven notebook to my chest, thinking about what Miss Omar said when she gave it to me.

That maybe one day, when I'm ready, I can show it to someone I trust.

I walk back upstairs slowly, my heart feeling like it's on fire. Nell is still sitting on the bed, waiting for me though, and so I take a deep breath, feeling tears sting at the corner of my eyes.

Nell doesn't blink when she takes it from me. And her face doesn't give anything away, even when she gets to the bit about Mum that Joel read out. And the terrible last line underneath that too, which I swore I'd never show to anyone.

I don't feel like a strong,
independent woman. I
feel scared and alone.
   I wish I had a mum
that didn't have PTSD.

I'm breathing very fast because I'm showing Nell the worst thing I've ever said, and even though it's the truth, it's not really. I love my mum, even though she isn't very well. It's just hard and I wish, wish, wish it wasn't.

Nell pinches her lips together. The crow looks at me and hops onto my shoulder, pecking at my hair. And then Nell drags me to her in a huge hug, so all I can smell is lavender soap and cakes and wet fur.

'You're as strong as the strongest ant, Nora. You wouldn't have shown this to me if you weren't.'

I feel strong – hugging her. I feel like finally I'm on dry land and can stand tall and unmovable.

She pulls away and holds my chin in her fingers. 'What you're feeling is completely natural and you mustn't feel scared or embarrassed. These are very big feelings to have on your own though.' I notice that her eyes are storm-cloud grey. 'Would it be okay if I helped you, Nora?'

Part of me still wants to shake my head and run away to the sea, where I can pretend that everything is *fine*. But it's not. And Nell feels like an unmovable rock in a ferocious sea. I let her anchor me.

I nod slowly. 'Okay,' I say.

28

Kwame stays in the bath until he's as wrinkled as Fox the dog, but when he comes out, he's smiling wide and dressed in my dad's old clothes.

'I don't think I've ever had a bath with that many bubbles in.'

Nell's laugh is loud and fills the landing. 'I'll make us some tea until your parents arrive.'

We both spin round on the spot, our mouths open. 'You called them?' we say together.

Nell rolls her eyes. 'Well, I'm not about to kidnap

you, am I? I called your mum, Nora, and spoke to Bill – he was going to pass the message along to Kwame's parents, I believe.'

'Are they angry?' Kwame says.

'Is Mum okay?' I say at the same time.

Nell smiles and looks at the clock at the top of the stairs reading half past four. 'Well, you can ask them yourselves soon.'

She plods down the stairs still laughing, as Kwame groans.

'Sorry, Nora, this was a really bad plan. It's all my fault. And now—'

But I take his hand. 'It's not your fault, Kwame. We found the reason why the animals were bringing us here, didn't we? So I can get help – for me and my mum.' I narrow my eyes at him. 'But you already knew that, didn't you?'

Kwame looks at me guiltily. 'Only because you're so much like my grandad, like I said before. And we're friends, Nora – we help each other.' A smile grows on his face. 'You've helped me be brave enough to have the first non-make-believe Otter Adventure I've ever had.' He holds my hand tight, before grimacing again. 'Mum is going to ground me for a hundred years though.'

We tiptoe downstairs as Nell is finishing the tea. Outside, the rain has stopped and the sky is turning slowly from black to blue again – the new sun showing us a wide garden out the back filled with a hotchpotch of cages and nets.

'Are there more animals outside?' I ask.

Nell looks out the window with us. 'Some. Most of them I brought into the house from the storm – but the bigger ones had to stay outside.'

I look excitedly at Kwame, who doesn't look sure that those types of animals should be in a garden at all.

'Can we go see them?' I ask.

Nell shrugs, pouring the tea. 'Take your coats.'

We splash out the back door, walking around the broken path through a garden almost as wild as Kwame's grandad's. All around are cages made out of driftwood hammered together with rusty nails, and aviaries made from huge fishing nets. Most of them are empty, but Kwame almost steps into an enormous pond, which startles an angry goose.

'This place is like a nightmare,' he says, panting.

I laugh. 'Why is it you don't like animals?'

He scrunches his nose. 'It's not that I don't like

them – it's that I don't really trust them. They're wild!'

I point at his socks. 'A strange thing for a boy in tiger-striped socks to be afraid of.'

He grins at me. 'Well, maybe I'm a bit wild too.'

He roars and chases me further up the garden and into a barn at the back, where there's a huge Highland cow with shaggy hair and big horns, as well as a small family of deer. Kwame starts drawing them in his book, including the shaved patch on the cow and the broken antler on one of the smaller deer.

'You're getting better at drawing animals as they are, and not as they are in fantasy stories,' I say, impressed.

He shrugs. 'Turns out that real things are just as interesting.'

I hear boots up the path and Nell stands next to us in the barn, her arms resting on the rusty gate that's keeping the animals in.

'What's wrong with all these animals that means they had to be rescued?' Kwame asks.

'Nothing's ever *wrong* with anyone,' she says, giving me a sideways glance. 'But the Highland cow was abandoned by someone who'd thought she'd make a nice pet, which is how many of these animals find their way here. She's coming along well though. The deer at the back came to me having had a run-in with a fence, but they're almost better now.'

'Are you going to release them back into the wild?' Kwame asks.

Nell looks at me again and then back at the house. 'Some of them, yes. Some of them wouldn't survive out there now, or have conditions that mean they'll soon be leaving us anyway – like the parrot in the kitchen. I have a few sanctuaries and zoos interested in taking some of them, but the others . . .' She smiles. 'Well, I suppose they'll just have to stay with me.'

Kwame is about to ask another question, when we hear a call from the house.

'Nora? Kwame?!'

'Your parents are here,' Nell says needlessly as my stomach drops. 'The lifeguard just dropped them off – I saw their lights.'

Kwame gives me a terrified look and he squeezes my hand as Nell laughs.

'I'll go speak with them – soften the blow for you,' she says, winking and trudging up the path.

She meets them at the house and my stomach tumbles like the sea to see Mum, standing with her arms hugged around her. Her long hair whips about her face, and although I can't see her expression from here, I can tell she's both angry and afraid.

I let go of Kwame's hand, running to her to try to make it better again, but Nell gets there first. I watch as she says something and throws her arms around Mum in a huge hug.

My thoughts are ducking and diving through my head like lost seals. Mum doesn't seem sure what to do at first, but Nell keeps talking and talking, and gradually Mum's arms come up to hug her in return until she's holding onto her tightly. And it's odd, because my brilliant, strong mum looks almost small in Nell's arms – like she's just a ten-year-old girl too.

'It's okay,' I hear Nell say to Mum. 'We're both stubborn old mules. But I'm here now. You're here now.'

Kwame grabs my hand again, pulling me away from the angry goose in the pond. He gulps as his own parents march towards him, his mum's braids out of their bun and whipping round her in the wind like she's a Storm Goddess, and his dad holding tight to all his brothers like they might run away, too.

'What on earth did you think you were doing?!' his mum says, pulling him away from me into a bone-crushing hug. 'Lying. Putting you and Nora in danger. Coming to a stranger's house miles away without leaving so much as a note?!' She lets him go to give him a stern stare. 'I'm extremely disappointed—'

'It was my idea,' I say, stepping in front of Kwame.

'No, it was mine,' he says, dragging me back.

We squabble until Kwame's dad sighs loudly. 'It doesn't matter whose idea it was – the point is that it was a stupid idea. We trusted you both and we're very, very disappointed.'

Kwame's shoulders slump. I've never seen his brothers so still, even though I can tell they're itching to go and see all the animals in the barn at the back.

The silence stretches until a teenage boy steps forward. I've not seen him before, but figure it must be Kwame's older brother Izaak, because he looks like a taller Kwame with a stubbly moustache.

'Pretty cool though,' he says. His parents glare at him and he holds his hands up. 'What? I'm just saying that this is scaredy-cat *Kwame* we're talking about. Breaking rules, somehow taking a train by himself and captaining a boat in the middle of a storm to some sort of hidden animal island? I mean . . .' He pats his brother on the back. 'Respect, Kwame.'

Kwame bites back a pleased smile and his mum starts lecturing again about safety and telling the truth, but I step away as I spot Mum coming up the path slowly with Bill staying behind to talk to Nell.

I wonder for a moment if she's going to explode at me again like she did before, because what I did today was much, much worse. I can see the lines on her face where her ghosts have been pulling at her. She looks tired and I have so much sorry in my bones, it feels like they're made out of elephants.

'Mum—'

'Let's go over here,' she says, gripping my hand tightly in her icy-cold one and walking with me slowly up the path past the barn.

I can feel Kwame's eyes on me, but I can hear his mum still lecturing him about responsibility, so I know he's not going to follow. Usually, that would make me feel better, because things are always better when it's just me and Mum – but right now I miss his hand in mine.

We don't speak, but the trees talk for us, rustling on winds we can't feel yet and sounding like the world is roaring mad at me. And I want to say sorry. I want to say that I was only trying to help. I want to say that I love her. But my mouth feels dry.

Mum doesn't say anything either, but holds my hand tightly. We walk down a hidden path, overgrown with brambles and bushes, with rocks jutting out and making huge puddles in our path. Mum finds a way through it all though, and then we're on the edge of the island. Instead of seeing land in the distance, all we see is the stretch of the wild grey sea. The clouds are still tumbling, smudging the line between them and the water, so it feels like we're standing on the edge of a new blank page.

'I used to come here with your dad,' she says, sitting down on a rock a little way from where the land disappears into the sea spray.

I sit down with her, watching a small crab at our feet scuttle into a rock pool. Mum never talks about Dad, so I keep quiet so there's space for her to say more.

'He was always a wild thing – your dad. We stayed here with Nell for a while when we met and you were born. I thought that cutting ourselves off from everyone else would tame him – bring him closer.' She smiles sadly. 'But we weren't right for each other. He wanted adventure and I wanted to use my degree.'

She's pale and skinny, but also strong as bone. She strokes the hair out of my face.

'I did it again, didn't I? I marooned us on our own little island to try to tame the wild things inside me.'

I hug her tight with one arm, her hoodie smelling of home. 'I like our own little island.'

She squeezes me back. 'Me too. But you know, it's probably not very good for us.'

I can feel the words building in my head and they hurt the bones in my hand somehow. And I'm afraid to say them. Afraid it will hurt her, when that's the last thing I ever want to do, ever.

Out the corner of my eye, I spot a rainbow shape trotting to a rock jutting out into the sea and turning its eyes on me.

The fox. The fox that first came to me in the middle of the night and changed everything.

The waves smash against the rock she sits on, but she doesn't blink and the sea spray doesn't make her fur wet. She tucks her bushy tail across her paws and nods at me in a way that says, *Be brave, Nora Frost.*

I suck in my breath. And I tell Mum the truth.

'When we saw the doctor, I thought I could make you better on my own. I thought I could be strong enough to keep everything the way it was. I thought I could pretend that everything was *fine*.' I take another deep breath. 'I don't think things are *fine* any more, Mum. I think we need some help.'

The words feel full of electricity, but Mum doesn't jump. She just keeps hold of me. 'Oh, Nora. I'm so sorry, love. It's been so hard to know how much to tell you about the PTSD. You've always been so grown up.' She squeezes me tighter. 'I never meant to put that pressure on you and I'm so sorry.'

I think she's crying and I think I am too. But the waves and the wind in the trees and the gulls calling to each other are too loud to know for sure. What I do know, is that Mum's got me. And I've got her.

'What would you say to having Nell come to stay with us for a while, at our house?'

I pull away, wiping my face on my sleeve. 'What about the animals?'

Mum laughs. 'Well, I'm not sure we'll have room for a cow in the garden, but we'll do what we can. It might be a nice distraction.'

My heart leaps. I look over to the fox on the rock, and her rainbow edges seem brighter than ever.

I look back at Mum. 'I do see ghost animals you know, Mum. They led me here. They knew Nell would be able to help us.'

Mum tucks my hair behind my ears, smiling. 'Well, however exciting that sounds, in future perhaps come to me before following ghosts to the edge of the world.'

I nod and my heart whoops. 'The fox is on that rock. Maybe you can see her rainbow edges now—'

I swing my head back to the sea and stop in my tracks, because she's gone. I jump up, looking around at the empty trees and grey waves, but see no trace of a red-rust tail disappearing.

Disappointment sinks in me. I was hoping that the fox at least would stay with me – to show me how to keep being brave and strong, like Mum.

Mum stands with me, looping her hand back in mine, and she points far out to the blurry horizon.

'I don't see a fox,' she says. 'But I do see a rainbow. Look.'

I look and I see it, too – faint but growing brighter and brighter. And it's a perfect arc, stretching across the blank-page sky and writing something new on it. Something hopeful and strong.

I smile. 'I see it, too,' I say.

29

I thought everything might change overnight, but Mum says these things can take a little while.

Nell has to find good homes for some of her animals, which is easy for some, like the Highland cow, which went to a special farm in Scotland. But for others like the owl, she has to spend a lot of time meeting people and making sure they're going to be properly looked after.

Meanwhile, Kwame and I are grounded, so we can only see each other at school. We find a way to speak though, using signs at the window when he's at his grandad's.

At school, I think a lot about
what Mum said about marooning
herself on her own little island, and so
I pull Kwame out of the tree as it starts to
blossom into a waterfall of pinks, and onto the
playground with the others. We play games that
Kwame's grandad taught him, like the Hare Race
and Guess the Raven. And it turns out there are a lot of
kids who are our kind of weird.

But just one other who wears tiger-striped socks
now, too.

'Joel!' Kwame calls, asking him to kick the ball to
him at football. Joel does – not aiming for his head this
time, but at his feet. And even though Kwame misses,
Joel laughs and smacks him on the back.

'You're rubbish at football.'

Kwame laughs too, giving up the game to sit with Saffie and me on the bench, drawing animals with rainbow edges.

'I'm better at drawing than you are though,' Kwame says, sketching a perfect Highland cow with his tongue out.

Miss Omar and Miss Rose stand behind us, and I know they're thinking about the fight we had just one month ago and how everything can change so quickly. But that's the thing about friendship – it can appear suddenly like a rainbow-lit ghost animal, and just like that the night doesn't seem as dark any more.

At home time, we say goodbye to Joel at his house, and Kwame rides us along the canal all the way home, cycling even slower than usual so we can spend more time together before we're back to being grounded again.

But soon we're out on our road and seeing a great big truck outside my house – Nell loudly shouting at people to be careful with the cages inside.

I jump off the back of the bike and run as fast as I can to her, wrapping my arms around her middle.

'Careful!' She laughs. 'I'm an old lady – you'll pull me over with hugs like that.'

But she's strong enough to take anything.

I grin at her. 'Are you finally moving in?'

She nods to the truck and I see Mum in the back, laughing with a dark-haired removal man as they try to wrestle a shouty one-legged seagull back into his cage. Her cheeks look pink and her laugh is loud. I hold Nell's arm, tight.

'How many animals are staying?'

'Eight,' she says. 'Plus Ethel, because I couldn't leave her by herself.'

I laugh and run into the house where the stuffed tiger is standing tall by the wide-open curtains.

And inside, our house is alive with wild animals the wild didn't want any more. The crow I met in my dad's old bedroom is on a perch in the garden, as Bill is assembling an aviary for it with Kwame's dad. There's no deer, but there is a tank with a spider in it behind the sofa, and a grey squirrel clinging onto the curtains.

I race upstairs to see if Kwame is in the window yet, when I see a fox curled at the bottom of my bed.

I freeze, blinking for the rainbow edges. Since I saw the ghost fox on the island last month, I've not seen one ghost animal anywhere. But this isn't a ghost – it's alive.

I crouch down, looking at her, and she untucks her chin from her tail to look at me too.

She's not the same as my ghost fox. She's older, I think, with scars hiding in her fur and one milky-white eye. I reach out my hand as a question and she sniffs at it, before resting her head back down and letting me stroke her.

This time, my hand touches wiry rust-red fur and I feel my heart soar.

'You're safe now,' I whisper to her. 'I'm Nora, and I'm here to help.'

The fox sighs, her eyes drooping like it's the end of a very long day. I stay with her for a long time, feeling my own eyes droop, until I hear my name from downstairs.

'Nora? We've got a surprise for you.'

I blink, wondering what could be more surprising than a fox on my bed. I stumble into the kitchen where Nell is holding her seagull again and somehow also chopping vegetables for a home-made lasagne.

She winks at me. 'In the garden.'

I race outside and see Bill and Mum and Kwame and his family, all crowded round something.

'Is it another Ethel?' I ask, smiling.

But then everyone steps back and there, standing tall and glistening-new in Bill's hands, is my own red bike, back from the dead.

I look between Mum and Kwame, breath hiccuping. This must be some kind of joke, because my bike is lost, gone. At the bottom of the canal.

There's a hand on my shoulder and it's Nell, pushing me forward.

I reach my fingers out and feel its very real metal frame and rubber grips and front suspension. It looks almost exactly the same as I remember, although it's got a new posh seat and a tiger-striped bell on the front.

I look to Mum, who is beaming. 'How?' I whisper.

Kwame whacks Bill on the back. 'Bill fished it out! He's been working on it at Grandad's for ages.'

Bill looks embarrassed. 'Well, I couldn't have done it without Kwame showing me where it was.'

I throw my arms round them both, saying 'thank you, thank you, thank you' over and over and over again.

Mum joins in the hug and so does Nell and so does the dark-haired removal man for some reason, who seems to be standing very close to Mum.

We squeeze each other and laugh, and at the centre of it all, I feel as strong as a thousand ants.

'Well, go on, then. Give her a test!' Kwame's dad calls.

I hop on shakily, trying out the new bell, which sends

the people and animals all cheering. I push off, feeling all my bones sink back into their old lines, and I don't think I could be smiling any wider.

Kwame races round to open the back gate to the alley that runs behind the houses.

I stop to let him climb onto the back before our parents can remind us that we're grounded.

Together, we ride down the alley, looping back onto my road and past his grandad's house, who waves at us from the window. And I feel myself floating up, up, up the faster we go.

'Ghost bike coming through!' Kwame sings, laughing.

The canal is calling me and the wilderness the other side of that. But for now I turn round at the end of the road and cycle back towards the crowd of people waiting for me outside my red front door.

'It's not a ghost any more,' I say, standing tall on my pedals. 'It's alive.'

The Night Animals

The most special things in our lives tend to have a habit of sticking around long after they've gone. They leave an imprint, a little like a ghost animal, that's both there and not there. We might glance them at the corner of our eye in a daydream, or find them hidden in the depths of our thoughts, lurking.

For Nora, these ghosts come when she needs them most. They show her that she's not alone and that asking for help can be transformative. And they take the shape of a fox, a hare, a raven, an otter and – once upon a time – a tiger called Ethel.

Although I'm not lucky enough to be visited by

animal spectres anymore (my imaginary childhood dog has long since got bored and wandered off), I continue to be haunted by stories. One story in particular followed me as I was writing this book. It's not my story, but the story of my Great Aunt Kathleen, who my grandma would delight my sister and I with tales of when we were kids. Apparently, my Great Aunt Kathleen had a fox in her conservatory, a fish in her bathtub, a seagull under her arm and even a monkey in her garden – to name but a few. Her whole house was given over to animals that needed her help and had nowhere else to go. It's a story I'd all but forgotten about until it came to me in the middle of the night, its claws pressed into my chest.

If there's one thing I learned with Nora when writing this book, it's to learn to recognise the ghosts when they come. Whether they're memories, thoughts or feelings – hauntings usually happen for a reason. They can help us recognise those parts of ourselves we bury deep down and remind us that we can be brave. If we follow them, we can open ourselves to finding new friendships. And when we're strong enough to tell someone about them, they can lead us to find the help we need to become even stronger together.

ACKNOWLEDGEMENTS

As always, I have a big list of people to thank – not only for making this book what it is, but for all the support I've received from booksellers, librarians, bloggers and teachers this past year. I'm so sorry I can't name you all, but please know that everything you do is truly appreciated.

First on the list here is Lucy Pearse, who saw exactly what this story should be and helped me find my way there. Also to Sharon King-Chai, who I'm so very grateful wanted to work with me again and created the most beautiful cover and inside illustrations (I continue to be your biggest fan). I also want to thank the entire team at Simon & Schuster Children's Books for being utterly brilliant, namely Olivia Horrox, Rachel Denwood and everyone in editorial, design, sales, marketing and rights.

Sallyanne Sweeney and all the team at Mulcahy Sweeney Associates – thank you for your continued hard work and support. I feel tremendously lucky to have you in my corner.

I want to thank the authors and other advance readers for their generous time and words (although apologies to Katya Balan that we couldn't include her whole blurb on the cover – next time). Author thanks also to Yasmin Rahman, Joseph Elliott, Aisha Bushby, Holly Jackson, Sam Copeland and Struan Murray, as well as my new S&S author friends and event buddies.

Annie Rose and David Speedman – thank you for being the most epic friends this past year. You are the best accidental part-time housemates. Anna Burtt – thank you firstly for being you (of course) and secondly for your online writing club that's responsible for at least ten thousand words of this book. Thanks as ever to Kathryn, Harriet and Anna; Hayley, Amy, Sabina and Adela; Pippa Lewis, and my brilliant supportive team at Oxford Saïd.

Mum and Dad – sorry it took this long to dedicate a book to you. They are, of course, all yours in one way or another. Same goes to my ever-supportive partner, Ryan; Louise, Jay, Amelia and Edward; as well as my grandparents and the entire Annis family. Chris – thank you for researching my family history so diligently and helping to bring the ghosts of the past back to life.

Finally – last but very much not least – thanks as always to you, reader. Not only did you read this whole book, but the acknowledgements too! You really do make this writing lark the very best job in the world.

ABOUT THE AUTHOR

Sarah Ann Juckes writes books for young people. Her YA debut *Outside* (Penguin) was nominated for the Carnegie Medal Award 2020, shortlisted for Mslexia's Children's Novel Award, and longlisted for the Bath Children's Novel Award 2017. Her second YA novel, *The World Between Us* was translated into several languages worldwide and published in March 2021. Her first middle grade novel, *The Hunt for the Nightingale*, was published to wide critical acclaim.

Sarah is a writing tutor, mentor and works for Oxford University. She lives opposite a graveyard on the edge of the Cotswolds with her partner and cat.

ABOUT THE ILLUSTRATOR

Sharon King-Chai is an award-winning designer and illustrator. Born in Australia, she moved to London in 2003 after completing an Honours degree in Visual Communication at the University of Technology Sydney, and has been based in north London ever since. Sharon has worked on a wide range of projects including album artwork, branding and logos, product packaging, book covers and event identities. Recent work includes collaborations with Julia Donaldson on the stunning and award-winning *Animalphabet* and *Counting Creatures*, as well as her solo picture book *Starbird*, winner of the Kate Greenaway Shadowers' Choice award 2021.

Turn the page to read an extract from
Sarah Ann Juckes' beautiful adventure:

The HUNT the for Nightingale

'Full of hope, beauty, and ultimately
a healing song to nature'
Hannah Gold, author of *The Last Bear*

Nightingale songs are made up of around two hundred different phrases

I don't like losing things. It makes my stomach hurt, and I feel dizzy and sick.

I seem to feel anxious like that more than anyone else in my school. Dad always tells me that I'm worrying over nothing. He always says things like: 'the other children in your class aren't really laughing at you, Jasper,' or that: 'losing your homework isn't the end of the world, you know'.

I'm not sure about that, because Rosie not being here feels like the end of everything, which is probably why I've felt so panicky all this week. But Mum's right – usually I can make the panic go away by thinking about good, true things instead, like everything in our *Book of Birds*.

The *Book of Birds* is a book that Rosie and I have been writing for ages and for ever, and it has everything we know about birds in it. It's the map of my brain, and it's filled with feathers and facts about how to find different types of birds. And when I read it, thoughts about birds take over the worry and I don't feel so bad any more.

There are pages and pages about the nightingale. They say that it's a 'migratory bird', which means it flies away in the summer and comes back to the field behind our house every April. And even though Rosie has flown off to university now because she's nine years older than me, she still promised to drive home every other weekend in April and May, so we could sit in our tree together and listen to the nightingale sing, because it's important.

Two weeks ago, when the nightingale hadn't arrived like it usually does, Rosie sat with me in the dark and the silence.

'I don't like it,' I said. 'The nightingale is usually here by now, isn't it? And now it's May and we've still not heard it once.'

She held my hand in the black. 'You know, I heard there was a nightingale at the M23 motorway services? I bet that's our bird, Jasper. I bet it just got lost on its way home. A bird is only missing until you find it. And I'll find it – I promise.'

And I couldn't really see her face, but Rosie always tells the truth. So I believed her.

'I'll help you,' I said.

And she squeezed my hand, tight. 'We'll do it together, me and you. I'll come back again next weekend.'

That's what she said. She even wrote it herself in our *Book of Birds*.

Rosie and Jasper's hunt for the nightingale

NEXT WEEKEND

She was supposed to come back last Friday – a whole week ago now. I kept looking at our drive after school, waiting for Rosie's rusty purple car to chug up the kerb, with its feathery seat covers and the sunshine music she always plays at full volume. But it was hard to keep a lookout, as Mum and Dad suddenly went out for a long time and left me with our granny, who lives across the road. Granny let me watch cartoons all weekend, but didn't answer any of my questions about where Mum, Dad or Rosie were and kept leaving me to go and sit in her bedroom for some reason.

Mum and Dad were gone so long that I thought maybe they'd got lost, too. And maybe they had, because when they finally came home, they looked as though they didn't know where they were. And Rosie wasn't with them.

I didn't like their expressions. They looked scared and it made me panic. They wanted to hug me and talk to me, but I couldn't listen because my stomach was hurting badly. When I feel anxious like that, the only thing that ever makes me feel like I'm not floating away on an angry, black sea – is birds.

So, while Dad cried, I thought about how nightingales fly three thousand miles to Africa every year.

And while Mum rubbed my hands between hers tightly, I thought about how common nightingales can also be found across Europe and Asia.

I felt bad about not listening properly, but I couldn't help it. I'm supposed to distract myself with nice thoughts when I feel panicky. But the only thing that was left in my head at the end was one thing Dad said:

'Rosie has gone to a Better Place.'

It should have been a nice thing to hear, but it was confusing. What place could possibly be better than sitting in our tree, listening to our nightingale? I am her Better Place.

So where is she?

I turn on my phone and dial her number again, listening to the crackle silence on the other end until her answering machine starts. And I do that again and again, until Mum comes in to say goodnight. But maybe I'm still mad at her for talking about the nightingale like it isn't important, because I pretend to be asleep.

She sits on my bed and watches me for ages. At some point, I do such a good job of pretending that I actually do fall asleep. But when I wake up the next morning, she's gone.

I jump out of bed and run outside still in my pyjamas to check the tree again. And when I can't find Rosie in the branches, I come back to search all the rooms in the house for the millionth time. But all I find is our cat, Fish, asleep on the bathmat.

I go downstairs and jump on the sofa in the living room, so I can pull back the curtains and look on the drive for Rosie's purple car again. But all I can see is the tangled-up front garden and an empty space on the drive next to Mum and Dad's car.

Dad comes in and he's wearing his jumper inside out. He sees me looking out the window and looks sad. 'Maybe we should get you back to school . . .'

I didn't go to school all last week. Mum said I didn't need to go if I didn't want to, and I never want to, so I didn't. It did get boring though – especially because I kept being sent to Granny's. And at her house, there was nothing to distract me from the stomach-ache feeling that something was very wrong.

'It's Saturday,' I say, sliding down the sofa.

Dad looks at his watch, surprised, and then comes to sit with me on the sofa, squeezing my shoulders really tight.

'You know your mum and I love you very much.'

I nod, because I do know that. But him saying it like that makes my heart feel fluttery for some reason, so I wiggle out of his grip and try to escape before he sees that I'm panicking again.

'Where are you going?' he calls as I get to the door.

I stop, but I don't look at him. 'I need to find out where the "Better Place" is,' I mumble.

Dad makes a strange noise in his throat. 'Probably with your silly birds, isn't it,' he says, bitterly.

I am about to argue that birds are magnificent and not silly, but then it clicks.

'Dad, you're a genius!' I leave him in the living room and run up the stairs to my bedroom, where I left our *Book of Birds*. I grab it from the bed and spin through the pages until I find it again.

NEXT WEEKEND

Dad's right. If Rosie isn't here with me, then her Better Place must be with the nightingale. And if the nightingale is at the motorway services like she said, now I know where to find her.

She told me last weekend that something is only missing until you find it. So if I can find them both, maybe everything will go back to normal.